TOP COW PRODUCTIONS PRESENTS

Created by

LINDA SEJIC, MATT HAWKINS & JENNI CHEUNG

Published by Top Cow Productions, Inc.
Los Angeles

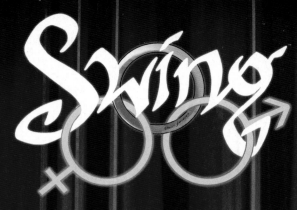

CREATED BY
Linda Sejic, Matt Hawkins and Jenni Cheung

WRITTEN BY
Matt Hawkins

ART BY
Yishan Li

LETTERING BY
Troy Peteri

BASED ON A STORY
AND CHARACTERS DEVELOPED BY
Linda Sejic
Stjepan Sejic
Matt Hawkins
Jenni Cheung

For Top Cow Productions, Inc.
Marc Silvestri - CEO
Matt Hawkins - President & COO
Elena Salcedo - Vice President of Operations
Vincent Valentine - Lead Production Artist

IMAGE COMICS, INC. • **Todd McFarlane**: President • **Jim Valentino**: Vice President • **Marc Silvestri**: Chief Executive Officer • **Erik Larsen**: Chief Financial Officer • **Robert Kirkman**: Chief Operating Officer • **Eric Stephenson**: Publisher / Chief Creative Officer • **Nicole Lapalme**: Controller • **Leanna Caunter**: Accounting Analyst • **Sue Korpela**: Accounting & HR Manager • **Marla Eizik**: Talent Liaison • **Jeff Boison**: Director of Sales & Publishing Planning • **Dirk Wood**: Director of International Sales & Licensing • **Alex Cox**: Director of Direct Market Sales • **Chloe Ramos**: Book Market & Library Sales Manager • **Emilio Bautista**: Digital Sales Coordinator • **Jon Schlaffman**: Specialty Sales Coordinator • **Kat Salazar**: Director of PR & Marketing • **Drew Fitzgerald**: Marketing Content Associate • **Heather Doornink**: Production Director • **Drew Gill**: Art Director • **Hilary DiLoreto**: Print Manager • **Tricia Ramos**: Traffic Manager • **Melissa Gifford**: Content Manager • **Erika Schnatz**: Senior Production Artist • **Ryan Brewer**: Production Artist • **Deanna Phelps**: Production Artist • IMAGECOMICS.COM

To find the comic shop
nearest you, call:
1-888-COMICBOOK
Want more info? Check out:
www.topcow.com
for news & exclusive Top Cow merchandise!

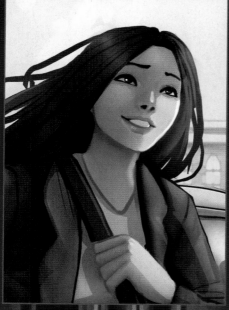

Cathy Chang

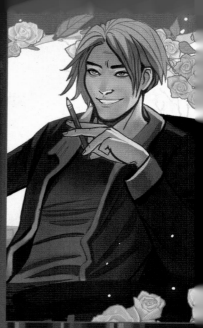

Dan Lincoln

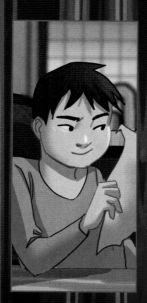

Blake Lincoln

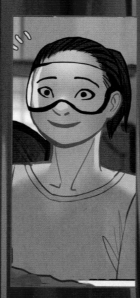

Ashley Lincoln

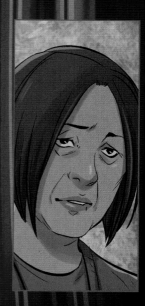

Mom

In the last two volumes of
Swing
DAN LINCOLN WAS A BRIGHT YOUNG GRAD STUDENT AND A GIFTED WRITER...
DETERMINED TO CRAFT THE NEXT GREAT AMERICAN NOVEL.
CATHY CHANG WAS A COLLEGE FRESHMAN, ON HER OWN AND CUTTING LOOSE FOR THE FIRST TIME IN HER SHELTERED LIFE.
WHEN THEY FIRST MET, SPARKS FLEW.
IT WASN'T LONG BEFORE THEIR "TUTORING SESSIONS" TURNED INTO SOMETHING ELSE...
AND WHEN THEIR FLING TURNED INTO SOMETHING DEEPER...
PREGNANT
NOT PREGNANT
THEY FOUND THEMSELVES FACING A NEW CHALLENGE - TOGETHER.
BUT FOR ALL THE FEAR THAT COMES WITH A SHOT-GUN WEDDING, DAN AND CATHY WERE HAPPY.
THEY BELIEVED IN EACH OTHER. WHAT-EVER CAME NEXT...
THEY COULD FACE IT TOGETHER.

BUT *8 YEARS* AND *TWO KIDS* LATER,
THE MAGIC STARTED TO FADE.

ROUTINE REPLACED ROMANCE.

RESPONSIBILITY

DAN STARTED *TEACHING* HIGH SCHOOL ENGLISH --

AND SPENT MORE TIME GRINDING AWAY AT RPGS THAN WRITING HIS NOVEL.

CATHY ENDED UP IN THE *ENTERTAINMENT INDUSTRY* --

COURTING CLIENTS AND MANAGING A TEAM OF WEB DESIGNERS AND ENGINEERS.

THE MORE THEY DRIFTED, THE MORE *TEMPTATION* LOOMED.

BUT THEY LOVED EACH OTHER.

THEY DIDN'T WANT TO FEEL THIS *RESENTMENT.*

THEY BOTH WANTED TO FEEL *CLOSER...*

THEY WOULD BECOME *SWINGERS.*

THEY WANTED TO FEEL *THE HEAT* AGAIN.

AND CATHY HAD A PLAN TO PUT THE SPICE BACK INTO THEIR MARRIAGE.

I THINK I'D LIKE TO TRY THAT.

THEY MADE RULES. THEY RESPECTED EACH OTHER'S BOUNDARIES.
AND AT FIRST, MERELY ENTERTAINING THE IDEA SEEMED TO BRING BACK THE OLD EXCITEMENT.
WHAT THE FUCK?
BUT DAN WAS SKEPTICAL AND INSECURE.
CATHY WAS PATIENT...
BUT SHE WORRIED THEIR MARRIAGE WAS ENDING BEFORE THEY COULD EVEN TRY OPENING IT UP.
SHE CONFIDED IN AN OLD FRIEND...
SO WITH DEBBIE'S HELP, CATHY HATCHED A PLAN.
NO STRANGERS, NO SPECIAL CLUBS --
JUST GOOD OLD-FASHIONED SEDUCTION.
IT WAS FAR FROM TRADITIONAL, BUT IT WORKED.
HERE WAS SOMETHING NEW, AND DAN AND CATHY LOVED IT.
AND LOVED EACH OTHER MORE FOR IT.

AFTER CATHY GOT DAN A SERIES OF THREESOMES WITH HER FRIENDS, HE WAS WILLING TO TRY A FOURSOME WITH ANOTHER COUPLE.
HI, GUYS. I'M MARY AND THIS IS MY HUSBAND CLINT. WE USE CHERI AND JACK UNTIL WE SEE THE COUPLE'S LEGIT.
FIGHTING THROUGH A SERIES OF FAKES AND FLAKES VIA THE SWINGERS' ONLINE DATING SITES, THEY FINALLY MET CLINT AND MARY, A COUPLE THEY BOTH LIKED, AND THEY HAD THEIR FIRST SUCCESSFUL COUPLES SWING.
DAN AND CATHY GOT MORE EXPERIENCE AND DAN LEARNED THAT HE MIGHT NEED VIAGRA FROM TIME TO TIME TO MAINTAIN HIS ERECTION BECAUSE OF THE ANXIETY IN THESE SITUATIONS.
ARE YOU OKAY? YOU'RE STILL NOT HARD.
NOT AT ALL. IT'S JUST A REGULAR FRIDAY, BUT I WANTED TO TREAT YOU TO A SPECIAL NIGHT OUT.
WANTING TO MAKE SURE THEIR RELATIONSHIP STAYED ROCK SOLID, THEY INSTITUTED REGULAR DATE NIGHTS FOR JUST THE TWO OF THEM.
THEIR COMMUNICATION, HONESTY AND SHARED EXPERIENCE RESULTED IN A RENAISSANCE IN THEIR RELATIONSHIP. LIFE WAS GOOD.

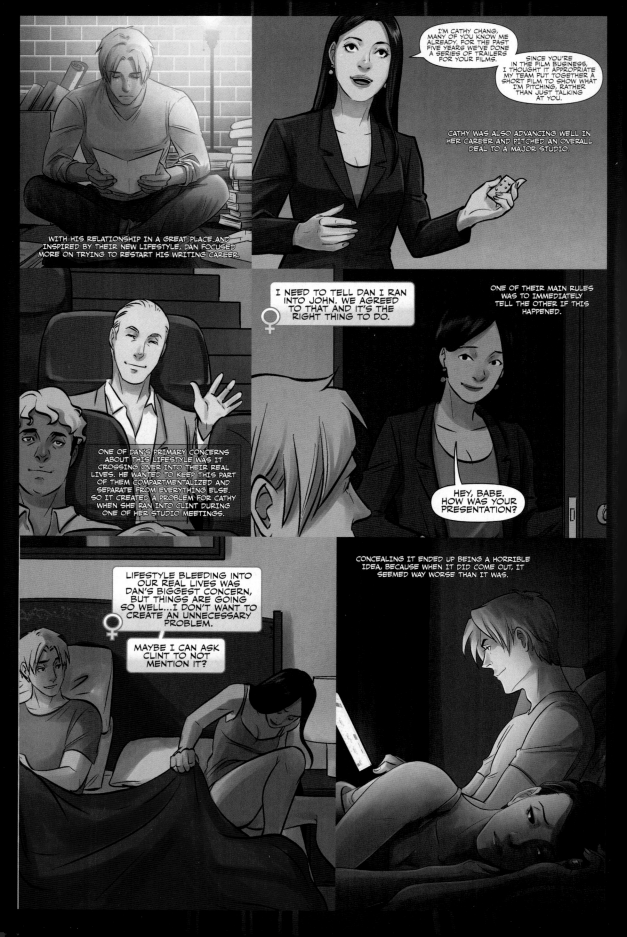

I'M CATHY CHANG, MANY OF YOU KNOW ME ALREADY. FOR THE PAST FIVE YEARS WE'VE DONE A SERIES OF TRAILERS FOR YOUR FILMS.

SINCE YOU'RE IN THE FILM BUSINESS, I THOUGHT IT APPROPRIATE MY TEAM PUT TOGETHER A SHORT FILM TO SHOW WHAT I'M PITCHING, RATHER THAN JUST TALKING AT YOU.

CATHY WAS ALSO ADVANCING WELL IN HER CAREER AND PITCHED AN OVERALL DEAL TO A MAJOR STUDIO.

WITH HIS RELATIONSHIP IN A GREAT PLACE AND INSPIRED BY THEIR NEW LIFESTYLE, DAN FOCUSED MORE ON TRYING TO RESTART HIS WRITING CAREER.

I NEED TO TELL DAN I RAN INTO JOHN. WE AGREED TO THAT AND IT'S THE RIGHT THING TO DO.

ONE OF THEIR MAIN RULES WAS TO IMMEDIATELY TELL THE OTHER IF THIS HAPPENED.

ONE OF DAN'S PRIMARY CONCERNS ABOUT THIS LIFESTYLE WAS IT CROSSING OVER INTO THEIR REAL LIVES. HE WANTED TO KEEP THIS PART OF THEM COMPARTMENTALIZED AND SEPARATE FROM EVERYTHING ELSE. SO IT CREATED A PROBLEM FOR CATHY WHEN SHE RAN INTO CLINT DURING ONE OF HER STUDIO MEETINGS.

HEY, BABE. HOW WAS YOUR PRESENTATION?

CONCEALING IT ENDED UP BEING A HORRIBLE IDEA, BECAUSE WHEN IT DID COME OUT, IT SEEMED WAY WORSE THAN IT WAS.

LIFESTYLE BLEEDING INTO OUR REAL LIVES WAS DAN'S BIGGEST CONCERN, BUT THINGS ARE GOING SO WELL...I DON'T WANT TO CREATE AN UNNECESSARY PROBLEM.

MAYBE I CAN ASK CLINT TO NOT MENTION IT?

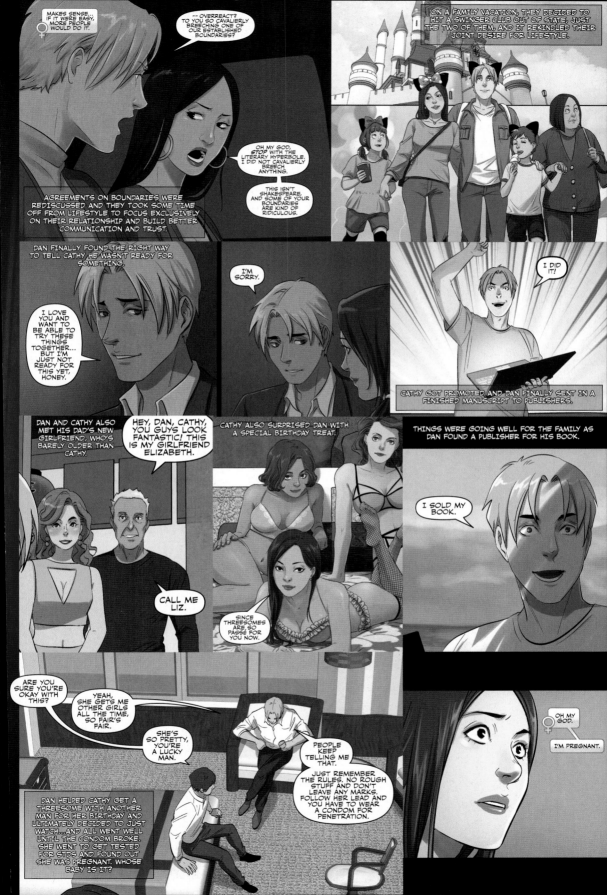

MAKES SENSE... IF IT WERE EASY, MORE PEOPLE WOULD DO IT.

-- OVERREACT? TO YOU SO CAVALIERLY BREECHING ONE OF OUR ESTABLISHED BOUNDARIES?

OH MY GOD, *STOP* WITH THE LITERARY HYPERBOLE. I DID NOT CAVALIERLY BREECH ANYTHING.

THIS ISN'T SHAKESPEARE, AND SOME OF YOUR BOUNDARIES ARE KIND OF RIDICULOUS.

AGREEMENTS ON BOUNDARIES WERE REDISCUSSED AND THEY TOOK SOME TIME OFF FROM LIFESTYLE TO FOCUS EXCLUSIVELY ON THEIR RELATIONSHIP AND BUILD BETTER COMMUNICATION AND TRUST.

ON A FAMILY VACATION, THEY DECIDED TO HIT A SWINGER CLUB OUT OF STATE, JUST THE TWO OF THEM, AND IT REKINDLED THEIR JOINT DESIRE FOR LIFESTYLE.

DAN FINALLY FOUND THE RIGHT WAY TO TELL CATHY HE WASN'T READY FOR SOMETHING.

I LOVE YOU AND WANT TO BE ABLE TO TRY THESE THINGS TOGETHER... BUT I'M JUST NOT READY FOR THIS YET, HONEY.

I'M SORRY.

I DID IT!

CATHY GOT PROMOTED AND DAN FINALLY SENT IN A FINISHED MANUSCRIPT TO PUBLISHERS.

DAN AND CATHY ALSO MET HIS DAD'S NEW GIRLFRIEND, WHO'S BARELY OLDER THAN CATHY.

HEY, DAN, CATHY, YOU GUYS LOOK FANTASTIC! THIS IS MY GIRLFRIEND ELIZABETH.

CALL ME LIZ.

CATHY ALSO SURPRISED DAN WITH A SPECIAL BIRTHDAY TREAT.

SINCE THREESOMES ARE SO PASSÉ FOR YOU NOW.

THINGS WERE GOING WELL FOR THE FAMILY AS DAN FOUND A PUBLISHER FOR HIS BOOK.

I SOLD MY BOOK.

ARE YOU SURE YOU'RE OKAY WITH THIS?

YEAH, SHE GETS ME OTHER GIRLS ALL THE TIME, SO FAIR'S FAIR.

SHE'S SO PRETTY, YOU'RE A LUCKY MAN.

PEOPLE KEEP TELLING ME THAT. JUST REMEMBER THE RULES. NO ROUGH STUFF AND DON'T LEAVE ANY MARKS. FOLLOW HER LEAD AND YOU HAVE TO WEAR A CONDOM FOR PENETRATION.

DAN HELPED CATHY GET A THREESOME WITH ANOTHER MAN FOR HER BIRTHDAY AND ULTIMATELY DECIDED TO JUST WATCH...AND ALL WENT WELL UNTIL THE CONDOM BROKE. SHE WENT TO GET TESTED FOR STDS AND FOUND OUT SHE WAS PREGNANT. WHOSE BABY IS IT?

OH MY GOD.

I'M PREGNANT.

NALLY! A FULL-BLOWN, HEH, ORGY AND WE'RE PARTICIPATING.
THE "DOUBLE LIFE" IS ONE OF THE FUN THINGS ABOUT BEING IN LIFESTYLE.
I CAN BE IN A PARENT/TEACHER CONFERENCE AT 6PM AND DOING THIS FOUR HOURS LATER.
THE NAUGHTY FACTOR, FOR ME, IS A DISTINCT TURN-ON.
AND DAN SEEMS TO BE INTO THE SWING OF THINGS.

I DO LIKE WATCHING DAN WITH OTHER WOMEN, THOUGH.
I THOUGHT COMPERSION MIGHT BE A MADE-UP WORD, BUT I GET IT NOW.

IT'S THE OPPOSITE OF JEALOUSY, WHICH DOES FLARE UP FOR ME AT TIMES.
JEALOUSY BREEDS SUSPICION, POSSESSIVENESS, ENVY, INTOLERANCE AND PRETTY MUCH NOTHING GOOD.
WHO WANTS THAT WHEN YOU CAN HAVE TRUST, INDEPENDENCE, GENEROSITY, FAIRNESS AND JOY?
AHHHH...
MOM.
MOM, ARE YOU ***AWAKE?*** I NEED HELP WITH MY HOMEWORK.
UH... BLAKE...

AHHH, REALITY... FUCK.
...DID YOU ASK YOUR DAD? YA KNOW... THE TEACHER? MOMMY WAS RESTING.
HE'S GAMING...AND IT'S MATH...YOU KNOW HE SUCKS AT MATH.
YEAH, HE DOES.
GIVE ME A FEW MINUTES AND I'LL MEET YOU DOWN-STAIRS.
THANKS, MOM.
EVER SMILE WHEN YOU WANT TO SCREAM?

IF DAN ACCIDENTALLY KNOCKED UP SOME GIRL, I'M NOT SURE HOW I'D HANDLE IT...
...BUT HE'S BARELY TOUCHED ME SINCE WE FOUND OUT, AND HE SPENDS ALL HIS FREE TIME GAMING.
I'D GET MAD ABOUT THAT...BUT GIVEN THAT I MIGHT BE PREGNANT WITH ANOTHER MAN'S BABY...I DON'T WANT TO ROCK THE BOAT.
I THINK IF WE COME IN FROM THE SOUTH ENTRANCE WE CAN SURPRISE THOSE GUARDS
WE'RE BOTH DEALING WITH IT IN OUR OWN WAY.

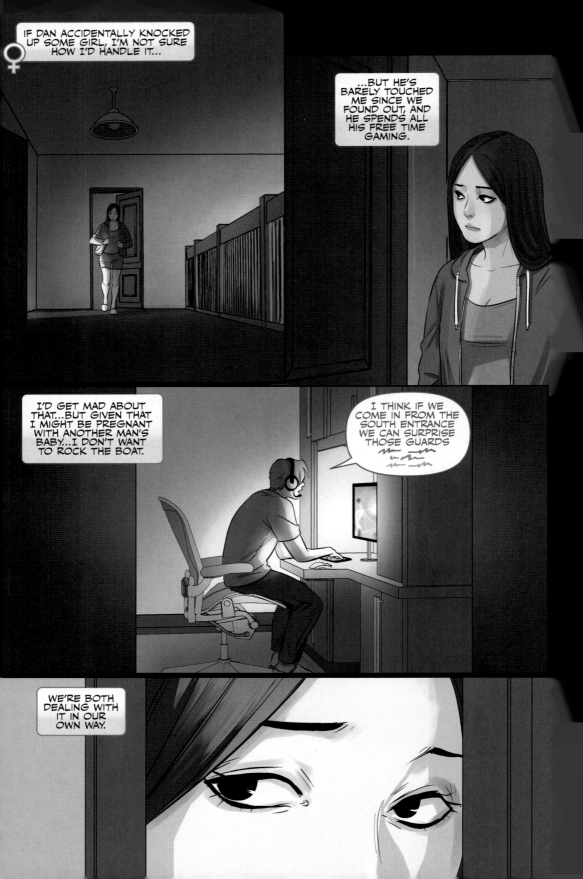

I TOOK A PATERNITY TEST, WE'VE BEEN WAITING FOR THE RESULT.
WE DISCUSSED OPTIONS BUT DECIDED TO WAIT UNTIL WE HAD ALL THE FACTS.
I'M PRO-CHOICE, BUT I'M NOT SURE I COULD ABORT MY BABY...EVEN IF IT'S NOT DAN'S.
MORE THAN ANYTHING, I'M JUST BUMMED.
WORK IS GOING WELL, CHRIST...I JUST GOT PROMOTED TO C.E.O. AND I'M ONLY TWENTY-NINE.
DAN AND I WERE FINALLY HITTING OUR GROOVE WITH THE LIFESTYLE STUFF...
...FAMILY'S GOOD.
I REALLY THOUGHT I COULD HAVE IT ALL.

AFTER TEN YEARS, I FINALLY LANDED A BOOK DEAL WITH A PUBLISHER.
YEAH, THEY'RE A SMALLER ONE, BUT THE BOOK IS REAL, AND I CAN ACTUALLY HOLD IT IN MY HANDS! HOW COOL IS THAT?
THIS IS THE THIRD BOOK SIGNING MY PUBLISHER SET UP.
THIS IS THE PART OF THE "DREAM" THEY DON'T TELL YOU ABOUT.
Victorian Fire
THEY DON'T WARN YOU NO ONE MIGHT SHOW UP.
I KNOW IT TAKES TIME TO BUILD AN AUDIENCE, BUT I NAIVELY ASSUMED THAT IF A STORE WANTED A SIGNING THAT MEANT THEY KNEW AT LEAST SOMEONE WOULD COME.
NOPE.
Victorian Fire
WELL, HI!
HEY, BABE, ARE WE EARLY? I THOUGHT IT WAS SUPPOSED TO START AT 2?

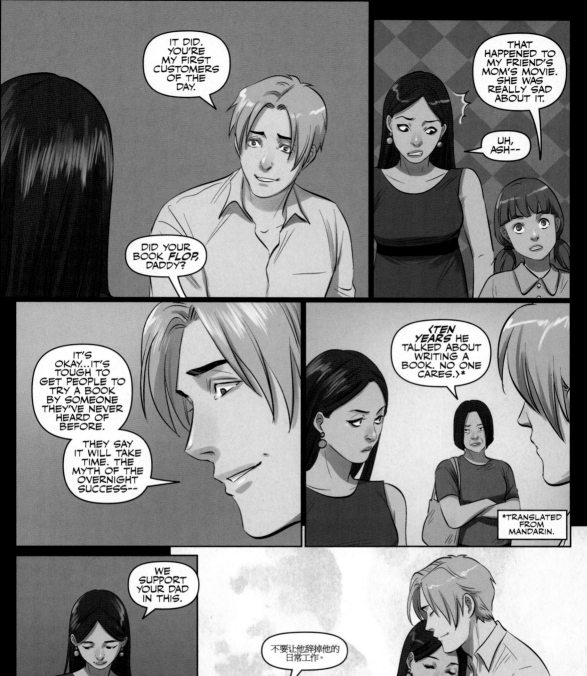

IT DID. YOU'RE MY FIRST CUSTOMERS OF THE DAY.

DID YOUR BOOK *FLOP,* DADDY?

THAT HAPPENED TO MY FRIEND'S MOM'S MOVIE. SHE WAS REALLY SAD ABOUT IT.

UH, ASH--

IT'S OKAY...IT'S TOUGH TO GET PEOPLE TO TRY A BOOK BY SOMEONE THEY'VE NEVER HEARD OF BEFORE.

THEY SAY IT WILL TAKE TIME. THE MYTH OF THE OVERNIGHT SUCCESS--

‹*TEN YEARS* HE TALKED ABOUT WRITING A BOOK. NO ONE CARES.›*

*TRANSLATED FROM MANDARIN.

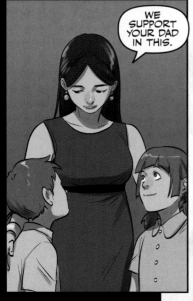

WE SUPPORT YOUR DAD IN THIS.

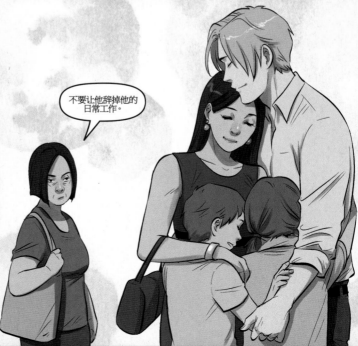

不要让他辞掉他的日常工作。

THE BOOK'S BEEN OUT FOR LESS THAN A WEEK NOW, REVIEWS ARE SOLID. THESE SIGNINGS, ALBEIT SPARSELY ATTENDED, BRING AWARENESS TO THE STORE STAFF, AT LEAST.
MR. LINCOLN? I'M VICKI, I'VE BEEN ASSIGNED TO TAKE CARE OF ALL YOUR NEEDS.
I BROUGHT YOU A BOTTLE OF WATER.
OH, THANKS. WHAT DO I OWE YOU?
FREE FOR AUTHORS... I REALLY ENJOYED YOUR BOOK, BY THE WAY.
THAT'S REALLY KIND OF HOT HOW HE CONVINCES BOTH OF THOSE GIRLS TO BE HIS LOVERS...
MY ROOMMATE AND I WISH WE COULD FIND A GUY THAT WOULD, YA KNOW, LET US LIVE WITH HIM AND WE COULD ALL HAVE A GOOD TIME.

RING
RING
WELL, I'M GLAD YOU ENJOYED IT. I'M WORKING ON ANOTHER BOOK NOW.
IS THIS ONE HOT TOO? I LOVE HOW SEXY
MY DOCTOR...
...OH MY GOD, OH MY GOD, OH MY GOD.
PLEASE BE DAN'S BABY.
HI, DOCTOR SINGH, IT'S CATHY.
I HAVE YOUR TEST RESULTS...
...THE BABY IS IN GOOD HEALTH AND THE FATHER IS YOUR HUSBAND.
ARE YOU SURE?
YES... THAT'S WHY WE RAN A DNA TEST.
OF COURSE, I'M SORRY... UH...THIS IS GREAT NEWS... THANK YOU... *THANK YOU!*

DAN!
THE DNA TEST RESULTS ARE IN...
...AND YOU *ARE* THE FATHER.
SORRY, I ALWAYS WANTED TO SAY THAT.

MA'AM, YOU CAN'T TOUCH THE AUTHORS.
THIS IS MY WIFE.
HAHAHAHAHA
<WHY ARE YOU SO HAPPY? HIS BOOK IS A FAILURE.>
WHAT'D SHE SAY?
THAT SHE'S HAPPY TO HAVE THE CHILDREN STAY OVER TONIGHT, SO WE CAN GO HOME AND PROPERLY CELEBRATE.

THERE'S SOMETHING ABOUT THE TOUCH OF AND INTIMACY WITH SOMEONE YOU TRULY LOVE THAT MAKES SEX WAY BETTER.
SOME THINK THAT GOES AGAINST THE SWINGER ETHOS...

...BUT THAT'S NOT TRUE AT ALL.
CUM IN ME.
SEX AND LOVE ARE TWO THINGS THAT GO GREAT TOGETHER.

I REALLY NEEDED THAT. YOU KNOW HOW HORNY I GET WHEN I'M PREGNANT.
I KNOW WE HAVEN'T TALKED ABOUT IT MUCH, BUT I THINK WE SHOULD TAKE A BREAK FROM SWINGING, MAYBE INDEFINITELY.
AND I SHOULD PROBABLY GET MY TUBES TIED WITH THE BIRTH...THE IUD I USE IS ONLY 99% EFFECTIVE AND YOU CUM IN ME THREE, FOUR TIMES A WEEK.
I CAN GET A VASECTOMY.
IF WE EVER DO LIFESTYLE AGAIN, LET'S HAVE THAT CONVO.
I ONLY EVER WANT TO HAVE *YOUR* BABIES.

AND THREE IS DEFINITELY ENOUGH HOOVERS TO FEED. GOOD THAT YOU GOT THAT PROMOTION, I DOUBT I'LL MAKE MORE THAN THE ADVANCE ON MY BOOK.
I'M SORRY, HONEY. I KNOW IT WAS YOUR DREAM.
I HAVE ALL I NEED.
RIGHT HERE.

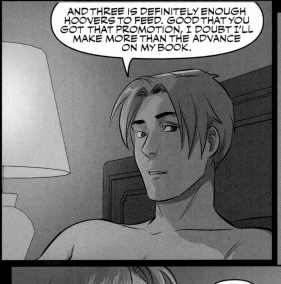

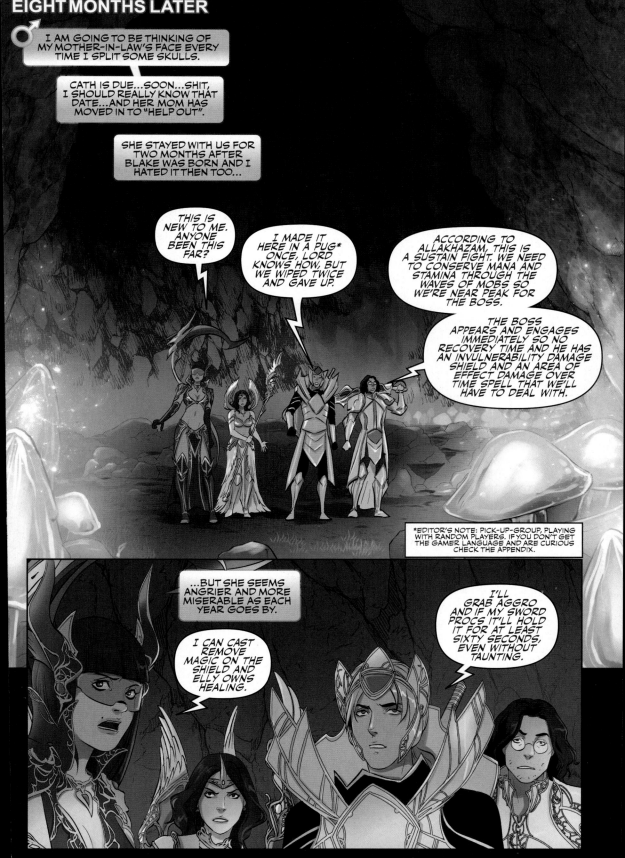

I AM GOING TO BE THINKING OF MY MOTHER-IN-LAW'S FACE EVERY TIME I SPLIT SOME SKULLS.

CATH IS DUE...SOON...SHIT, I SHOULD REALLY KNOW THAT DATE...AND HER MOM HAS MOVED IN TO "HELP OUT".

SHE STAYED WITH US FOR TWO MONTHS AFTER BLAKE WAS BORN AND I HATED IT THEN TOO...

THIS IS NEW TO ME. ANYONE BEEN THIS FAR?

I MADE IT HERE IN A PUG* ONCE, LORD KNOWS HOW, BUT WE WIPED TWICE AND GAVE UP.

ACCORDING TO ALLAKHAZAM, THIS IS A SUSTAIN FIGHT. WE NEED TO CONSERVE MANA AND STAMINA THROUGH THE WAVES OF MOBS SO WE'RE NEAR PEAK FOR THE BOSS.

THE BOSS APPEARS AND ENGAGES IMMEDIATELY SO NO RECOVERY TIME AND HE HAS AN INVULNERABILITY DAMAGE SHIELD AND AN AREA OF EFFECT DAMAGE OVER TIME SPELL THAT WE'LL HAVE TO DEAL WITH.

*EDITOR'S NOTE: PICK-UP-GROUP, PLAYING WITH RANDOM PLAYERS. IF YOU DON'T GET THE GAMER LANGUAGE AND ARE CURIOUS CHECK THE APPENDIX.

...BUT SHE SEEMS ANGRIER AND MORE MISERABLE AS EACH YEAR GOES BY.

I CAN CAST REMOVE MAGIC ON THE SHIELD AND ELLY OWNS HEALING.

I'LL GRAB AGGRO AND IF MY SWORD PROCS IT'LL HOLD IT FOR AT LEAST SIXTY SECONDS, EVEN WITHOUT TAUNTING.

I TRY TO JUST IGNORE HER.
TAUNT, TAUNT AND TAUNT AGAIN! IF YOU LOSE AGGRO, HE'LL ONE SHOT ELLY AND WE'RE DONE.
BUT IT'S HARD WHEN SHE'S HERE ALL THE TIME AND HAS NOTHING TO DO *BUT* BE NOSEY AND COMPLAIN ABOUT EVERYTHING.
WE GOT THIS. DAN HASN'T F'ED UP IN A LONG TIME.
LET'S DO IT!
I'M NOT STUPID.
I KNOW SHE BITCHES TO CATHY ABOUT ME ALL THE TIME.
WHO DISTURBS MY SLUMBER?
IT'S THE ONLY TIME THEY TALK IN MANDARIN.

BUT I FEIGN IGNORANCE FOR CATHY'S SAKE.
SLASH
BUT WHEN SHE GIVES ME THAT, "YOU RUINED MY DAUGHTER'S LIFE BY KNOCKING HER UP SO YOUNG" LOOK, I ENVISION HER FACE MELTING LIKE THE NAZIS AT THE END OF *RAIDERS*.
THAT WAS *BADASS!*
CAN YOU LIFT YOUR FEET?
UH, SURE... SORRY.
IT IS ENTIRELY POSSIBLE I'M OVERTHINKING AND EXAGGERATING ALL THIS...BUT COME ON.
CATH IS REALLY BUSY WITH HER JOB AND I'M BUSY TOO...UH...WITH MY BOOK SEQUEL THAT I...UH... *AHEM*...NEED TO START.
I'M GOING TO OWN YOU SO BAD.
WE'LL SEE.

SLSSSH
CATHY'S ONLY TAKING TWO MONTHS MATERNITY LEAVE...AND SHE'LL BE ON THE PHONE CONSTANTLY EVEN WHEN HOME, SO MAYBE I SHOULD APPRECIATE THE HELP.
SSHNK
IS THAT THE LAST?
YEAH, BOSS TIME.
IT'S JUST HARD WHEN I FEEL LIKE SHE HATES ME.
GAME FACES EVERYONE! THIS IS THE CULMINATION OF THREE WEEKS' WORTH OF RAIDING.

THIS IS ONE OF THE REASONS I LOVE GAMING SO MUCH.
FOR YOUR INSOLENCE, YOUR SOULS WILL REMAIN HERE WITH ME FOREVER!
READY CHECK.
READY.
ALWAYS.
READY.

PLAN, COMMUNICATE AND EXECUTE.
YAAAA!
WE ALL KNOW OUR PART AND WORK TOGETHER FOR A COMMON GOAL... AS SILLY AS IT MAY BE.
MY MAIN FUNCTION IN THE GROUP IS TO BE A MEAT SHIELD "TANK" AND HAVE THE MOBS HIT ME INSTEAD OF THE LESSER ARMORED AND SQUISHIER PLAYERS.
YOU'RE A BIG FAT CHEATER.
YOU'RE JUST A SORE LOSER, I NEVER CHEAT.
YES, YOU DO.
I DON'T HAVE TO, TO PWN SOMEONE AS BAD AS YOU.
KLICK KLICK KLICK KLICK
OUR GROUP DYNAMIC WORKS WELL AND I KNOW WHEN THE OTHER PLAYERS HATE ME...
NOW IS MY TIME TO SHINE.

...IT'S NEVER AN UNKNOWN, LIKE YOU-KNOW-WHO HERE.
I'M GETTING HEAVY LAG.
HELLO?
THIS IS KARMA.
HEY, THE WIFI IS DOWN.

GRANDMA, DID YOU UNPLUG THE ROUTER?
THE WHAT?
THE BLACK BOX THERE, WITH THE LITTLE ANTENNAS.
I DUNNO. SORRY IF I DID, I WAS JUST TRYING TO CLEAN UP.
YEAH, YOU DID. I'VE GOT IT.
YOU LUCKED OUT THERE, I WAS ABOUT TO OWN YOU SO BAD.
LET'S GO THEN, SHIT-FOR-BRAINS.
ASH, LANGUAGE.
MY MOTHER-IN-LAW IS A BITTER, LONELY OLD WOMAN DESPERATELY CLINGING TO HER DAUGHTER TO HAVE A LIFE...BUT SHE DOES HELP US ALL THE TIME.
SHE COOKS, CLEANS AND BABYSITS AND WE'RE NEVER WORRIED WHEN THE KIDS ARE WITH HER. WE KNOW THEY'RE SAFE.
I HAVE A PRETTY AWESOME LIFE. MY BOOK HAS PICKED UP IN SALES AND MY DEADLINE FOR THE SEQUEL IS ONLY MONTHS AWAY...BUT I HAVEN'T STARTED.
I NEED TO STOP GAMING SO MUCH AND GET TO WORK.

BEING A PARENT IS HARD, AND CATHY IS A WONDERFUL WOMAN. THAT *DOES* SPEAK VOLUMES ABOUT HER MOTHER.
MY BOOBS ARE SO *HUGE!* YOU THINK I SHOULD GET IMPLANTS NEXT YEAR TO KEEP THEM THIS SIZE?
I MET HER FATHER AT OUR WEDDING...AND HAVE NEVER SEEN OR SPOKEN TO HIM SINCE.
YOU CAN IF YOU WANT, BUT WHO'RE YOU TRYING TO IMPRESS?
YOU... AND ME, OF COURSE... I WANT TO LOOK GOOD WHEN I LOOK IN THE MIRROR.
HE MARRIED ANOTHER WOMAN IN CHINA BARELY OLDER THAN CATHY AND SHE HAS A HALF-BROTHER YOUNGER THAN ASHLEY SHE'S NEVER MET.
YOU SQUEEZE THREE FOOTBALLS OUT YOUR BUTT AND SEE IF IT AFFECTS *YOUR* FIGURE.

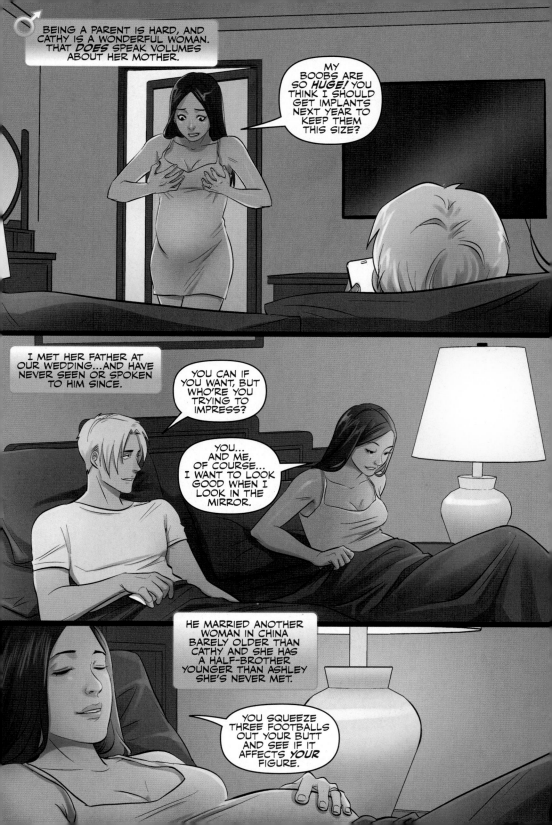

I GIVE MY POPS A LOT OF GRIEF, BUT AT LEAST HE'S STILL IN THE PICTURE, AND HAS MET HIS GRANDCHILDREN.
I WANTED TO TALK TO YOU ABOUT YOUR MOM.
THIS AGAIN? WE AGREED SHE COULD STAY FOR THREE MONTHS. WE'RE GOING TO NEED THE HELP...WHAT'D SHE DO?
NOTHING, I THINK MAYBE WE CAN DO SOMETHING NICE FOR HER FOR ALL SHE DOES.
OOOOKAY... WHAT DID *YOU* DO?
NOTHING. HEH, I'VE JUST BEEN THINKING ABOUT FAMILY. I NEVER REALLY THOUGHT ABOUT HOW HARD IT MUST HAVE BEEN FOR HER WHEN YOUR DAD JUST...*LEFT* LIKE THAT.
I LOVE MY DAD, BUT HE WANTED SOMETHING EVERY CHINESE FATHER WANTS...A *SON*... AND MY MOM COULDN'T GIVE THAT TO HIM.
SHE TRIED, YA KNOW, SHE HAD LIKE SEVEN MISCARRIAGES AFTER ME.

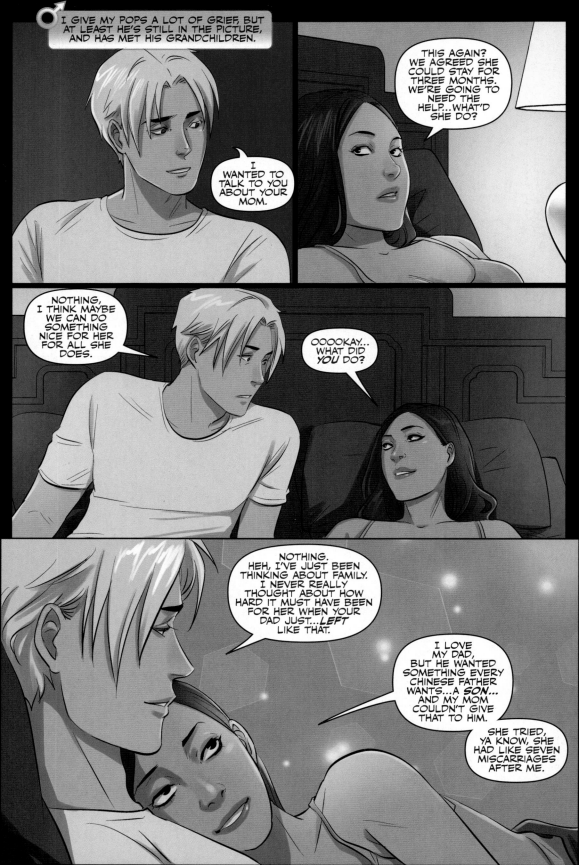

MAYBE YOU BROKE HER.
DON'T JOKE ABOUT THAT, PLEASE, I KNOW SHE THINKS THAT SOMETIMES.

FAMILY IS EVERYTHING.
I'LL TRY HARDER WITH YOUR MOM. GET SOME REST.

SIX MONTHS LATER
I SHOULD HAVE GOTTEN THE BOOB JOB...
...THEN THE EXTRA INCHES ON MY HIPS WOULD LOOK PROPORTIONATE AND I WOULDN'T NEED TO WORK OUT LIKE THIS.
SIXTY-HOUR-A-WEEK JOB...THREE FRICKIN' KIDS...NEEDY HUSBAND, LONELY MOM...HOW DO PEOPLE KEEP UP WITH IT ALL?
I BARELY SEE MY FRIENDS ANYMORE.
I KEEP UP WITH THEM BY READING THEIR INSTAGRAM POSTS.

TIME JUST ROLLS BY, DOESN'T IT?
I KNOW MY SITUATION IS UNUSUAL IN THIS DAY AND AGE.
CAN'T BELIEVE I'M GOING TO BE *THIRTY* NEXT MONTH.
I SHOULD STILL *FEEL* YOUNG... BUT I *DON'T.*
MY FRIEND DEBBIE WANTED TO TAKE ME TO VEGAS FOR MY DIRTY THIRTY, BUT I HAVE A HARD TIME HANGING OUT WITH HER FOR MORE THAN ABOUT AN HOUR AT A TIME ANYMORE.
SHE JUST FEELS SO...WHAT'S A NON-JUDGMENTAL WORD? SUPERFICIAL? FLIPPANT?
NAH, THOSE ARE BOTH PRETTY JUDGEY.
HER LIFE AND CONCERNS ARE SO DIFFERENT FROM MINE. SHE'S WORRIED ABOUT WHAT SHE'S GOING TO WEAR TO COACHELLA...
...I'M FIGURING OUT 529 INVESTMENT ACCOUNTS SO MY KIDS WILL HAVE COLLEGE FUNDS.

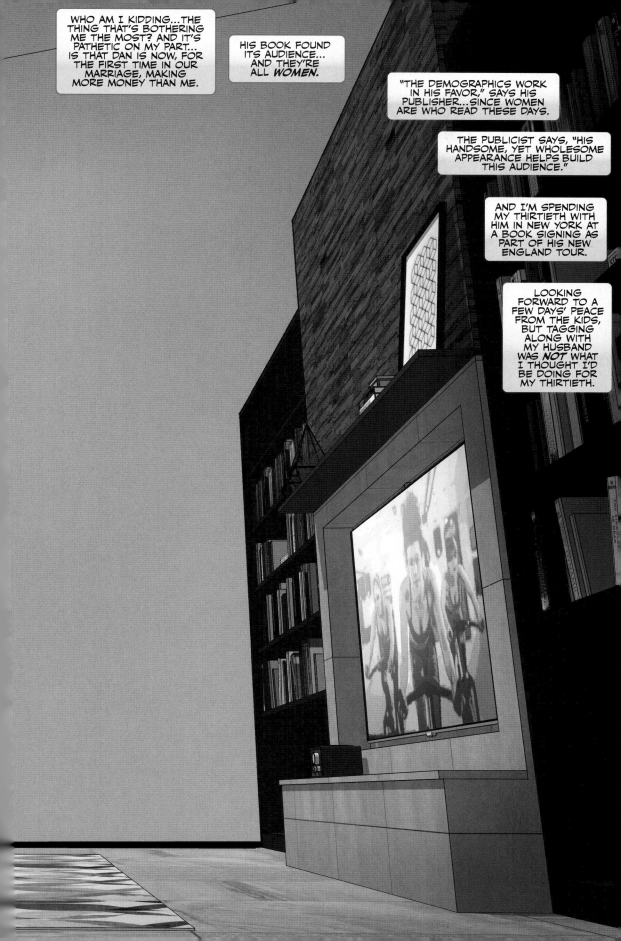

WHO AM I KIDDING...THE THING THAT'S BOTHERING ME THE MOST? AND IT'S PATHETIC ON MY PART... IS THAT DAN IS NOW, FOR THE FIRST TIME IN OUR MARRIAGE, MAKING MORE MONEY THAN ME.

HIS BOOK FOUND ITS AUDIENCE... AND THEY'RE ALL *WOMEN.*

"THE DEMOGRAPHICS WORK IN HIS FAVOR," SAYS HIS PUBLISHER...SINCE WOMEN ARE WHO READ THESE DAYS.

THE PUBLICIST SAYS, "HIS HANDSOME, YET WHOLESOME APPEARANCE HELPS BUILD THIS AUDIENCE."

AND I'M SPENDING MY THIRTIETH WITH HIM IN NEW YORK AT A BOOK SIGNING AS PART OF HIS NEW ENGLAND TOUR.

LOOKING FORWARD TO A FEW DAYS' PEACE FROM THE KIDS, BUT TAGGING ALONG WITH MY HUSBAND WAS *NOT* WHAT I THOUGHT I'D BE DOING FOR MY THIRTIETH.

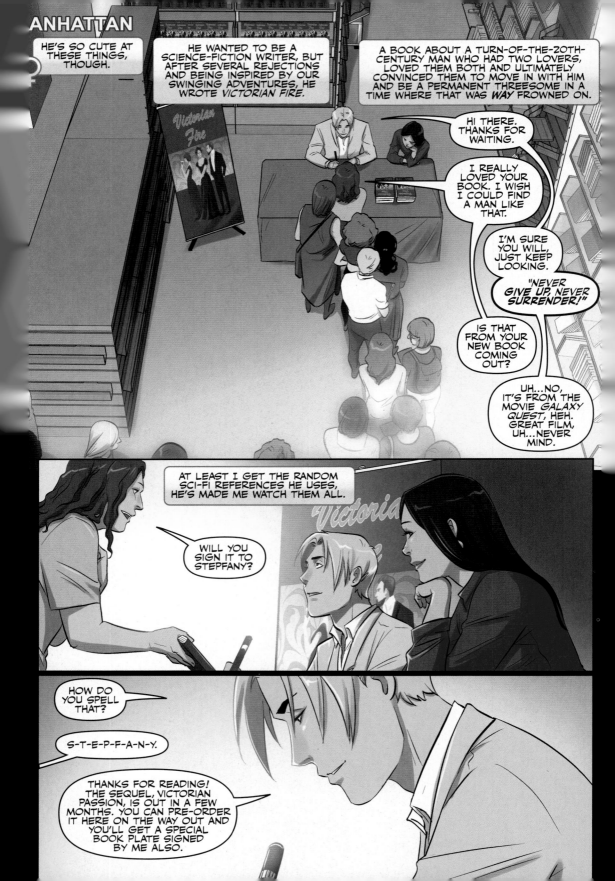

HE'S SO CUTE AT THESE THINGS, THOUGH.

HE WANTED TO BE A SCIENCE-FICTION WRITER, BUT AFTER SEVERAL REJECTIONS AND BEING INSPIRED BY OUR SWINGING ADVENTURES, HE WROTE *VICTORIAN FIRE*.

A BOOK ABOUT A TURN-OF-THE-20TH-CENTURY MAN WHO HAD TWO LOVERS, LOVED THEM BOTH AND ULTIMATELY CONVINCED THEM TO MOVE IN WITH HIM AND BE A PERMANENT THREESOME IN A TIME WHERE THAT WAS *WAY* FROWNED ON.

HI THERE. THANKS FOR WAITING.

I REALLY LOVED YOUR BOOK. I WISH I COULD FIND A MAN LIKE THAT.

I'M SURE YOU WILL, JUST KEEP LOOKING. *"NEVER GIVE UP, NEVER SURRENDER!"*

IS THAT FROM YOUR NEW BOOK COMING OUT?

UH...NO, IT'S FROM THE MOVIE *GALAXY QUEST*, HEH. GREAT FILM, UH...NEVER MIND.

AT LEAST I GET THE RANDOM SCI-FI REFERENCES HE USES, HE'S MADE ME WATCH THEM ALL.

WILL YOU SIGN IT TO STEPFANY?

HOW DO YOU SPELL THAT?

S-T-E-P-F-A-N-Y.

THANKS FOR READING! THE SEQUEL, VICTORIAN PASSION, IS OUT IN A FEW MONTHS. YOU CAN PRE-ORDER IT HERE ON THE WAY OUT AND YOU'LL GET A SPECIAL BOOK PLATE SIGNED BY ME ALSO.

ON THE PLUS SIDE: AFTER THIS, WE'RE GOING TO AN S&M CLUB THAT ONE OF HIS GAMER BUDDIES FREQUENTS. WE HAD DINNER WITH HER LAST NIGHT. SHE SEEMS NICE, MAYBE A LITTLE INTENSE.
CURIOUS ABOUT S&M...NEVER *TRIED* THAT.
EXCUSE ME...
...DO YOU KNOW IF DAN'S SINGLE OR NOT? SORRY IF THAT'S WEIRD, JUST THOUGHT YOU WERE HIS ASSISTANT OR SOMETHING, AND MIGHT KNOW.

YEAH, HE'S MARRIED... TO *ME.*
LIKE IT SAYS ON THE BACK OF THE BOOK.
OH! I'M SO SORRY.
YOU'RE A LUCKY GIRL, HE MUST BE FUN IN BED.
THANKS.
AND I'VE GOT THE STRETCH MARKS TO PROVE IT.

SOME OF THESE GIRLS ARE PRETTY BOLD.
I'D NEVER HAVE THE STONES TO SAY THAT TO ANOTHER WOMAN I'VE NEVER SPOKEN TO BEFORE ABOUT HER HUSBAND.
AND I BANG OTHER WOMEN'S HUSBANDS ALL THE TIME...OR I USED TO, SIGH.
I MISS LIFESTYLE.
IT IS MY BIRTHDAY WEEK, YOU KNOW. YOU BETTER WINE, DINE AND GIVE ME MULTIPLE ORGASMS LATER.
IN THE SPIRIT OF OUR COMING ADVENTURE, YES, MISTRESS.

S&M...UGH. I TRY TO KEEP AN OPEN MIND, BUT THIS ONE SCARES ME.
WE WENT TO DINNER LAST NIGHT WITH MY GAMING FRIEND ALLY.
SHE HAD READ MY BOOK AND HAD A LOT OF "QUESTIONS" SINCE SOME OF THE PASSAGES SEEMED "AUTHENTIC."
CATHY, AFTER A FEW GLASSES OF WINE, OUTED US, OF COURSE, AND WE TALKED ABOUT SWINGING FOR A WHILE.
ALLY SAYS EVERYONE HAS THEIR KINK AND PEOPLE SHOULDN'T BE ASHAMED OF IT IF IT'S ADULT AND CONSENSUAL, AND MENTIONED SHE FREQUENTED A S&M CLUB IF WE WANTED TO GO.
I READ THE REVIEWS ONLINE FOR THIS PLACE AND IT SEEMS AMAZING.
THERE ARE A FEW NEGATIVE ONES, BUT IT LOOKS LIKE THEIR OBJECTION IS ON MORAL GROUNDS.
REMINDS ME OF SOME OF MY BOOK REVIEWS.
THE BUTTERFLIES IN MY GUT REMIND ME OF THE FIRST TIME WE VISITED THAT LIFESTYLE CLUB IN L.A.
AND OH! THERE'S A SWINGER CLUB JUST A FEW BLOCKS OVER.
IF THIS IS A BUST, YOU WANT TO GO CHECK IT OUT?
BE FUN TO JUST LOOK AROUND. WE DON'T HAVE TO *DO* ANYTHING.
SURE, THAT *DOES* SOUND FUN.

WHAT'S SHIBARI?
NO CLUE.
HOW DOES IT FEEL?
MMMMMM

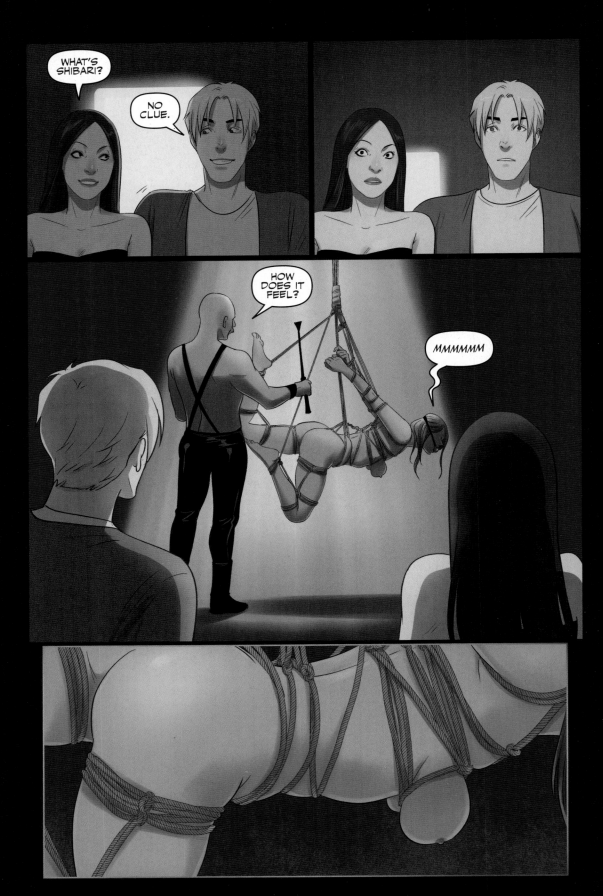

I'M GOING TO PULL IT TIGHTER.
MMMM
WONDER HOW SHE SAYS HER SAFE WORD WITH A BALL GAG IN HER MOUTH.
SHOULD WE HAVE ONE OF THOSE?
PROBABLY A GOOD IDEA.
WHACK

HOW ABOUT ALBATROSS?
TOO LONG. LET'S GO WITH RED.
WANT TO SPANK ME, BIG BOY?
SHOW ME WHO'S BOSS.
OH... OKAY.
TAP

HARDER!
WHACK
OH!
USE YOUR BELT.
AS YOU WISH.
GALAXY QUEST AND NOW PRINCESS BRIDE? NERD.
THWACK
AHHHH!

ALBATR... $@#¢**¢%#... RED!
ARE YOU OKAY?
YOU HIT MY CLIT... GOD, THAT REALLY STINGS.
HAHAHA HOLY FUCK! I'M HAVING COLLEGE FLASHBACKS RIGHT NOW.
SERIOUSLY THOUGH! YOU REALLY GOTTA EASE INTO THIS STUFF GRADUALLY. TRUST ME- SPEAKING FROM EXPERIENCE.
IT'S A BIT OF A LEARNING PROCESS.
I WANT TO LEARN.
UH, ME TOO... I GUESS. I'M SORRY, BABE.
I'M KIND OF SCARED TO HIT YOU NOW.

COME WITH ME, I'LL HAVE A FRIEND OF MINE SHOW YOU SOME BASICS.
THANKS, I LIKE BEING SUBMISSIVE, BUT I'D LIKE TO TRY SOME STUFF ON DAN, TOO.
YOU MIGHT BE A SWITCH. THAT'S SOMEONE WHO LIKES TO BOTH DOM AND SUB.
I'M GOING TO MAKE YOU MY BITCH.
ENTER THE SANCTUM...
FEISTY! I LIKE HER! DAN...

...OF MISTRESS MICHELLE.
SHE IS A DEAR FRIEND AND ONE OF THE BEST.
SHE DOESN'T TAKE NEWBIES, BUT SHE'S DOING ME THIS FAVOR, SO DON'T MAKE ME *LOOK* BAD.
COME IN.

UH, HELLO, MISTRESS.
THANKS, ALLY.
OF COURSE! AND SINCE MY GAMING BUDDY HERE HAS KILLED US MANY TIMES WITH HIS "WIFI" PROBLEMS, PLEASE MAKE IT *HURT* A BIT FOR ME.

TWO HOURS LATER
I'M GOING TO BE IN PAIN FOR DAYS.
OH, COME ON, I THOUGHT YOU WERE A BIG, STRONG MAN.
SERIOUSLY... BRUISES?
CAN'T TAKE A LITTLE *PAIN?*
I OBVIOUSLY CAN. THAT'S WHY I DIDN'T SAY THE SAFEWORD, BUT YEAH...
...I REALLY DON'T THINK THIS S&M STUFF IS FOR ME.
I DON'T THINK IT'S FOR ME EITHER, BUT I DON'T WANT TO MISS RIBBING DAN FOR A WHILE.
IT'S MY BIRTHDAY WEEK AFTER ALL!
LET'S GO BACK TO THE HOTEL, YOU CAN CLEAN UP, AND WE'LL GO TO CHECK OUT THAT LIFESTYLE CLUB.
I CAN PUT SOME FOUNDATION ON THOSE BRUISES... I WANT TO CHANGE ANYWAY.
YES, MISTRESS.

I'M GLAD WE'RE HERE. I WAS AFRAID DAN WOULDN'T WANT TO GET BACK INTO LIFESTYLE. I HOPE HE WANTS TO PLAY.
I KNOW CATHY HAS BEEN SHY ABOUT HER POST-PREGNANCY BOD, I WONDER IF I COULD GET HER TO PLAY?
HOW LATE DO YOU WANT TO STAY?
DUNNO, WE'RE STILL ON L.A. TIME AND I'M CLEAR ALL MORNING. JUST SOME PRESS STUFF IN THE AFTERNOON... WHAT TIME'S YOUR FLIGHT?
NOON.
YOU EAGER TO GET BACK TO THE KIDS?
YES AND NO. I'VE ONLY BEEN GONE A COUPLE DAYS, BUT I'M FEELING SOME SEPARATION ANXIETY FROM BABY LUKE. I SPOKE TO MY MOM, THEY'RE ALL FINE.
SHE GAVE ME GRIEF OVER THE FORMULA THING, BUT WHATEVER. I BREASTFED THAT BITER FOR ALMOST SIX MONTHS, MY NIPPLES NEED THE BREAK.

YOU WANT TO *PLAY?*
JINX! ONE, TWO, THREE.
THAT MEANS I CAN'T TALK, RIGHT? SO...YOU WANT MY MOUTH TO STAY CLOSED THE REST OF THE NIGHT?
I DEFINITELY DON'T WANT THAT. YOUR MOUTH HAS MANY FINE USES.
I LOVE YOU, CATH...I'M AMAZED AT HOW EASILY YOU SHED THAT POST-BABY WEIGHT. YOU LOOK HOTTER THAN EVER.
AWW, THANKS, LOVE. IT'S ONE OF THE ADVANTAGES OF HAVING BABIES SO YOUNG...AND I'M GLAD THAT ONE WILL BE MY LAST.

SHALL WE GET NAKED?
YES, PLEASE.
WOOHOO!

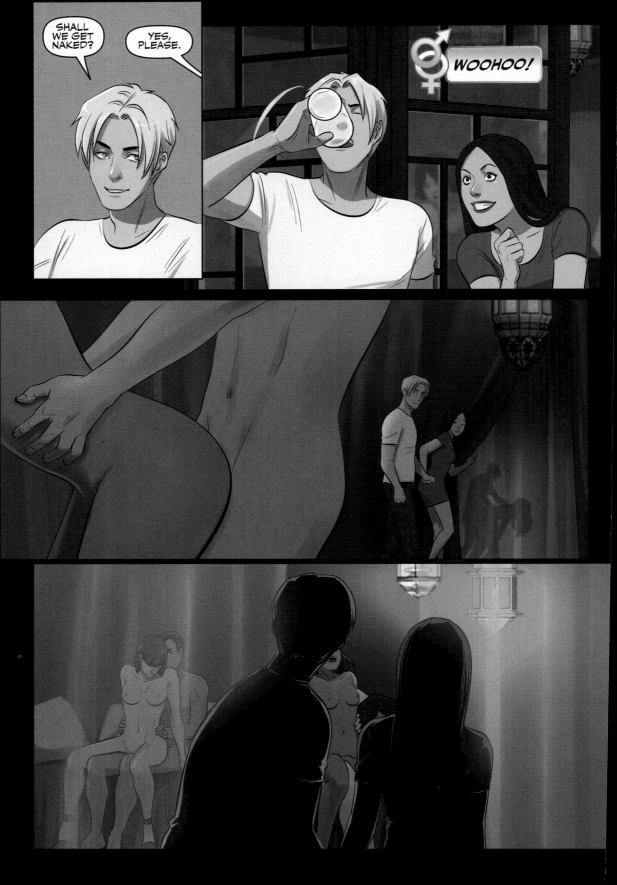

YOU WANT TO FIND A DARK CORNER SOMEWHERE?
THAT DOESN'T SOUND FUN AT ALL.
BUT *THAT* DOES.
I'VE NEVER USED A SEX SWING BEFORE, CAN WE TRY IT?
ANYTHING FOR YOU.

I THINK THIS IS HOW IT GOES.
WOW.

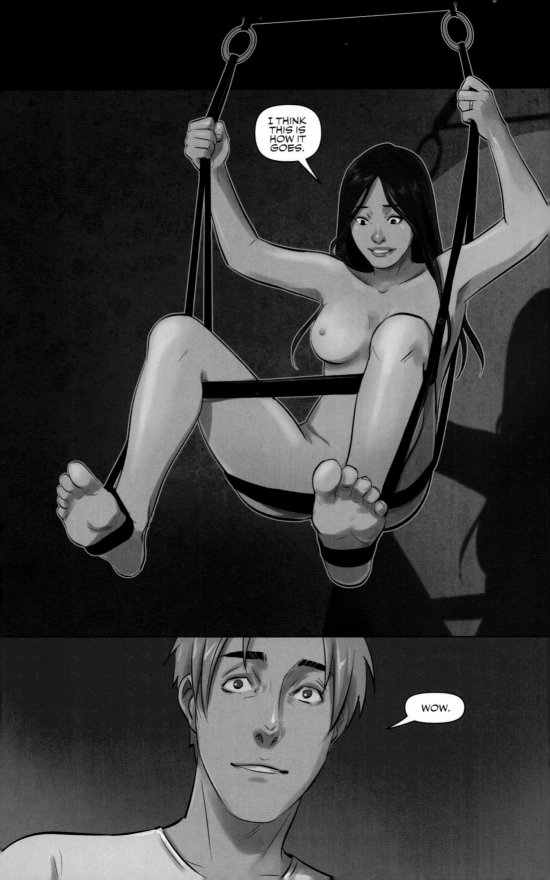

IT'S BEEN ALMOST TWO YEARS SINCE WE HAD SEX IN A PUBLIC PLACE. MY EXHIBITIONIST STREAK SEEMS TO STILL BE STRONG.
I HOPE THIS IS A FIRST STEP IN OUR GETTING BACK INTO THE REAL SWING OF THINGS.
I LOVE DAN WITH ALL MY HEART, AND IT'S HARD TO EXPLAIN TO SOME PEOPLE WHY I WANT TO SWING.
YOU WANT TO HEAD BACK TO THE HOTEL?
NOT YET, I LOVE THIS SONG.
I DON'T CARE IF PEOPLE KNOW WE SWING, BUT IT *IS* INTERESTING THE TWO TYPES OF REACTIONS I GET WHEN PEOPLE FIND OUT.
I WANT TO DANCE FOR YOU.
THEY'RE EITHER SUPER INTERESTED AND WANT TO KNOW ALL THE DETAILS.
OR THEY'RE SUPER JUDGMENTAL AND *STILL* WANT TO KNOW ALL THE DETAILS.
DAN IS MY ROCK, MY LIFE PARTNER, MY HUSBAND, THE FATHER OF MY CHILDREN AND MY BEST FRIEND.

MY FAVORITE MEAL IS A FIVE GUYS LITTLE BACON CHEESEBURGER ALL THE WAY WITH CAJUN FRIES AND A DIET COKE, BUT I WOULDN'T WANT THAT EVERY DAY.
HAH, I'D BE SO FAT.
VARIETY IS INDEED THE SPICE OF LIFE...AND WHY NOT?

WE LIVE WHAT...EIGHTY YEARS, IF WE'RE LUCKY?
SHOULDN'T WE TRY AND SQUEEZE AS MUCH JOY AND PLEASURE IN AS WE CAN?
AND IF THE MAN I LOVE, WHO LOVES ME, IS INTO IT...THEN AGAIN...I ASK WHY NOT? WHO ARE WE HURTING?
WHY NOT EXPERIENCE AS MUCH AS POSSIBLE IN THIS LIMITED WINDOW OF LIFE WE GET?
YOU ARE SO BEAUTIFUL.

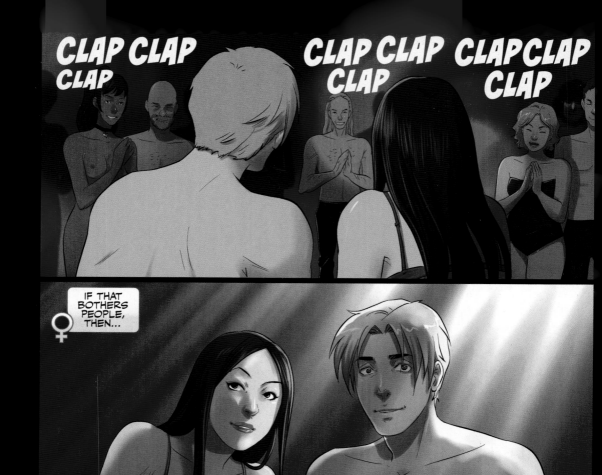

CLAP CLAP CLAP

CLAP CLAP CLAP

CLAPCLAP CLAP

IF THAT BOTHERS PEOPLE, THEN...

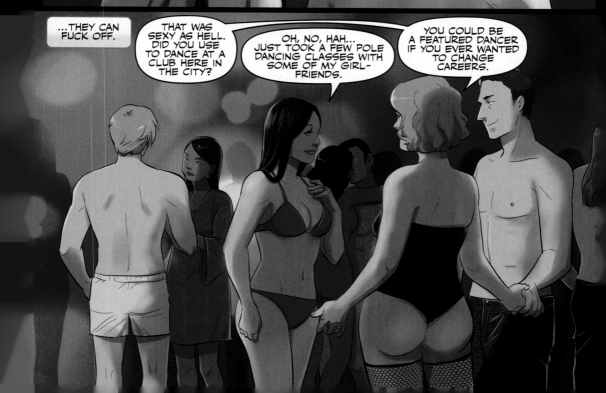

...THEY CAN FUCK OFF.

THAT WAS SEXY AS HELL. DID YOU USE TO DANCE AT A CLUB HERE IN THE CITY?

OH, NO, HAH... JUST TOOK A FEW POLE DANCING CLASSES WITH SOME OF MY GIRL-FRIENDS.

YOU COULD BE A FEATURED DANCER IF YOU EVER WANTED TO CHANGE CAREERS.

ONE MONTH LATER
SANTA MONICA, CALIFORNIA
YOU READY FOR THE PARTY TONIGHT? THE HALLOWEEN ONE IS SUPPOSED TO BE HUGE.
SHOULD BE FUN.
I'M LOOKING FORWARD TO SEEING THE "SLUTTY" VERSION OF EVERY COSTUME IMAGINABLE.
THERE'S A CONTEST FOR THAT. YOU COULD TOTALLY WIN.
GURGLE GURGLE
LUUUKKE.
OH MY GOD, DON'T "I AM YOUR FATHER" HIM AGAIN.
GURGLE... AWOOO.

BLAKE, ASH! DON'T GRAB MORE THAN ONE PIECE EACH, DON'T BE GREEDY.
REGRET LETTING ME PICK THE NAME NOW?
NO, YOUR NERDINESS IS CUTE.
IS BLAKE TALLER THAN ASHLEY NOW?
ALMOST, BUT DON'T SAY ANYTHING TO HER. SHE HATES IT.
YOU MAKE BEAUTIFUL BABIES.
I KNOW... GOOD THING THEY TAKE AFTER ME.

WAAAHHHH!
DEFINITELY TAKE AFTER YOU.
WAAHHH!
HEY. BUDDY, DON'T BITE...I'VE GOT PLANS FOR THOSE LATER.
WAAHHH!
MOMMY'S HERE.
COME HERE, BABY.

WHAT TIME IS YOUR MOM COMING OVER?
SHE SHOULD BE THERE NOW. SHE WANTS TO TEACH THEM ABOUT TENG CHIEH... IT'S A CHINESE HALLOWEEN THING AND IT TAKES TIME TO SET UP.
Quinny

YOU THINK SHE'D TEACH ME, TOO?
I THINK SHE'D LIKE THAT. YOU'VE NOT SHOWN MUCH INTEREST IN OUR TRADITIONS IN THE PAST.

MIDNIGHT
HALLOWEEN AND NEW YEAR'S EVE ARE THE TWO HOLIDAYS THE SWINGER LIFESTYLE EMBRACES TO THE MAX.
THE CLUBS GO ALL OUT, AND THE "ANNUAL SWINGERS" AND "LOOKIE-LOOS" SHOW UP.
Lifestyle Club
WE'RE SOLD OUT, IF YOU DON'T ALREADY HAVE A TICKET.
WE DO.
IT'S UNDER DAN LINCOLN.
OH... YOU'RE THE GUY.
SHEILA!
YOU ARE ON MY LAST NERVE, CARL. YOU KNOW HOW CRAZY TONIGHT IS.
OH! IT'S YOU.

I'M SORRY?
I'M A HUGE FAN OF YOUR BOOK! WHEN I REALIZED YOU AND YOUR WIFE WERE MEMBERS, I'VE BEEN WAITING FOR YOU TO COME BACK.
WE'LL COMP THE TICKETS IF YOU'LL SIGN HER BOOK.
Victorian Fire
HAPPY TO.
I'VE BEEN WAITING FOR THIS. YOU TWO HAVE NOT BEEN HERE IN A LONG TIME.
WE, UH, HAD A BABY...SO WE TOOK A BREAK.
I PRE-ORDERED YOUR NEXT ONE. CAN'T WAIT.
THAT'S A FIRST. I'VE NEVER HAD SOMEONE HIT ME UP OUTSIDE OF A BOOKSTORE SIGNING.

WE'VE NOT BEEN TO ONE OF THESE HALLOWEEN PARTIES BEFORE, BUT CLINT AND MARY GAVE US THEIR PERSPECTIVE... AND IT'S NOTED THEY ARE *NOT* ATTENDING.
WOW, IT'S PACKED.
THEY COMMENTED THAT THE LOOKIE-LOOS WHO COME ARE OFTEN VOYEURS AND NOT ACTUAL SWINGERS, AND THAT THE ONCE-A-YEAR "ANNUALS," WHO ONLY SWING ON HALLOWEEN OR NEW YEAR'S, ARE APPARENTLY MORE ANNOYING TO DEAL WITH.
I'M HOPING WE CAN FIND PEOPLE WE CLICK WITH TO PLAY. IT'S BEEN A LONG TIME!
WANT TO CHECK OUT THE PLAYROOMS?
YEAH, LET'S GO.

I HOPE WE CAN FIND A SPOT.
THIS HALLWAY WORKS.
DO YOU THINK THAT WOMAN THERE IS *HORNY?*
YOU GOOF, THERE'S ROOM OVER THERE.
WE DON'T WANT TO BE LATE...
"...FOR A VERY IMPORTANT DATE."

I THINK THAT COUPLE IS EYEING US.
NAVY AND THE BUNNY?
YEAH.
WOULD YOU LIKE TO PLAY WITH US?
WHAT DO YOU THINK, HATTER?
I'D HAVE TO BE MAD TO SAY NO.

I'M BUNNY.
I CAN SEE THAT. I LIKE THE EARS.
I MEAN, MY REAL NAME IS BUNNY.
EVEN BETTER.

DAN, WAKE UP.
SORRY, DRIFTED OFF FOR A SEC.
WE'VE NEVER DONE TWO DIFFERENT COUPLES BACK-TO-BACK LIKE THAT.
NOW WE HAVE.
FINISH ME, PLEASE.

THAT WAS A GOOD ONE.
I COULD TELL.
LET'S GO HOME.
OH MY GOD.

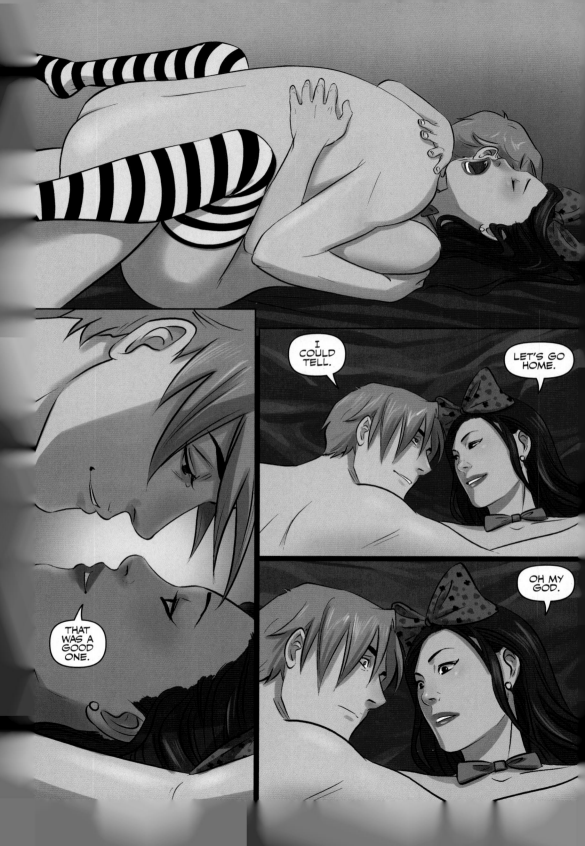

DAD?
WELL, THIS IS AWKWARD.

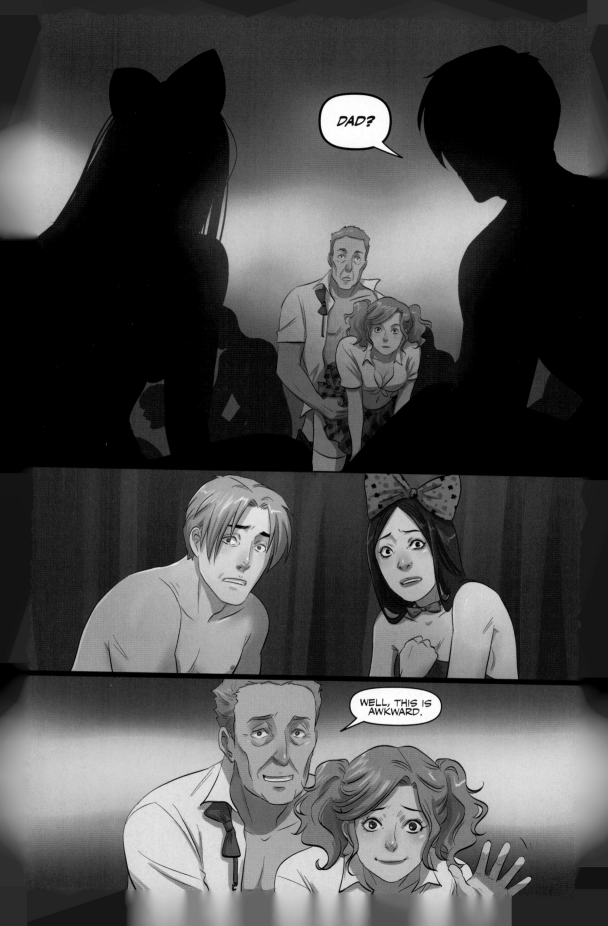

PARENTS ARE ALWAYS INTERESTING TO DEAL WITH.
YOU GET WHO YOU GET.
RUNNING INTO DAN'S DAD AT THE CLUB WAS...HEH...LET'S JUST SAY WE ALL AGREED TO PRETEND LIKE IT NEVER HAPPENED.
SO, WE'RE AT A CROSSROADS HERE. TRADITIONAL MOVIE MARKETING NO LONGER WORKS WITH STREAMING AND EVERYTHING GOING ON...
...WE EITHER CHANGE WITH THE TIMES OR WE--
CATHY, SORRY TO INTERRUPT.
IT'S URGENT... IT'S YOUR MOTHER.
<YOUR FATHER DIED. THEY'RE FLYING HIS BODY HERE, HE WANTED TO BE BURIED HERE NEXT TO HIS BROTHER AND HIS FAMILY IS HAVING A FUNERAL CEREMONY. THEY'D LIKE US BOTH TO COME.>
OF COURSE.
<I'M SORRY YOU'VE LOST YOUR FATHER.>

<YOU WILL TRY AGAIN. IT IS YOUR DUTY.>
<THE DOCTOR SAID ANOTHER MISCARRIAGE MIGHT KILL ME. I GAVE YOU ONE CHILD, THAT SHOULD BE ENOUGH.>
<I WANT A SON.>
DAD!
I LOVE MY FATHER, BUT HE WAS A COMPLICATED MAN.
MY MOTHER WENT ON TO HAVE TWO MORE MISCARRIAGES BEFORE HAVING TO HAVE AN EMERGENCY HYSTERECTOMY TO SAVE HER LIFE.

HE WAS A GOOD FATHER TO ME BUT WAS OVERLY LENIENT WHILE MY MOTHER WAS INSANELY STRICT.
THAT MIXED MESSAGE WAS TOUGH TO DEAL WITH AS A CHILD.
AFTER ME AND DAN'S WEDDING, HE LEFT MY MOTHER AND MOVED BACK TO CHINA, MARRIED A WOMAN HALF HIS AGE, AND HAD A SON THAT I'LL MEET TODAY FOR THE FIRST TIME...UGH.
<BOHAI CHANG LIVED A BLESSED LIFE AND HAD TWO CHILDREN. HIS BELOVED SON LEI CHANG AND HIS DAUGHTER CATHY CHANG. BOTH ARE WITH US HERE TODAY.>
MY MOTHER ONLY EVER HAD ONE MAN IN HER LIFE.
THEY MET WHEN SHE WAS FOURTEEN AND SHE'S HAD HIS NAME EVER SINCE.

<THAT'S HIS WIFE... MEI...AND THEIR SON LEI.>
<YOU ARE LUCKY TO HAVE A MAN LIKE DAN.>
<HE WON'T LEAVE YOU.>
<YOU GAVE HIM TWO SONS.>

CATHY?
<HI. SORRY TO BOTHER YOU, BUT I AM YOUR FATHER'S WIFE, AND THIS IS HIS SON. MAY I SPEAK WITH YOU?>
GIVE ME A MINUTE.
CAN YOU HELP ME CHANGE THE BABY?
<IT IS NICE TO FINALLY MEET YOU.>
<HE WANTED US TO COME TO THE U.S. MANY TIMES, BUT WE HAD FINANCIAL TROUBLES.>
<HIS WISH WAS FOR YOU TO KNOW YOUR BROTHER.>

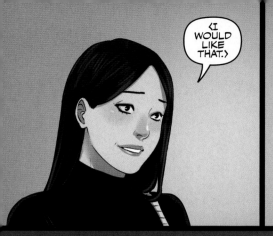

‹I WOULD LIKE THAT.›

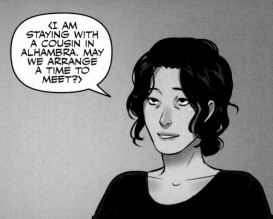

‹I AM STAYING WITH A COUSIN IN ALHAMBRA. MAY WE ARRANGE A TIME TO MEET?›

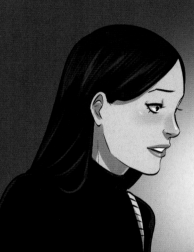

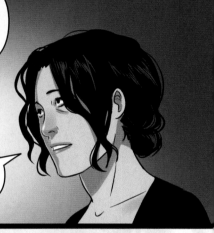

‹THAT'S KIND OF FAR. WOULD IT BE OKAY IF I GOT YOU A HOTEL ROOM CLOSER TO WHERE WE LIVE? LEI MIGHT LIKE THAT, IT'S CLOSE TO THE BEACH.›

‹THAT WOULD BE NICE. YOU ARE VERY KIND.›

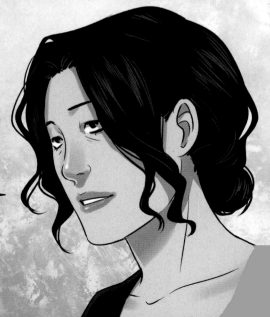

‹I WAS AFRAID YOU WOULD REJECT ME. YOUR FATHER WAS ALSO VERY KIND. I AM A FARMER'S DAUGHTER FROM WESTERN XINJIANG. YOUR FATHER SHOWED ME A BETTER LIFE AND I AM HAPPY THAT MY SON IS RECEIVING AN EDUCATION.›

‹HE WISHED WE COULD BE FRIENDS, BUT HE KNEW THAT YOU WOULD NOT ACCEPT ME, SINCE WE ARE THE SAME AGE.›

<WE CAN BE FRIENDS AND I WOULD LIKE TO KNOW MY BROTHER.>
<I WOULD ALSO LIKE TO HEAR MORE ABOUT MY FATHER'S LIFE IN CHINA.>
<I HAVE NOT SEEN HIM FOR ELEVEN YEARS. WE SPOKE ON THE PHONE, BUT-->
OW!
WHAT THE HELL?
<LEI, NO!>
<DO NOT SPEAK ILL OF MY DAD!>
WHOK
<I AM SORRY, HE IS A WILLFUL CHILD. YOUR FATHER WOULD NOT DISCIPLINE HIM.>
<WE CAN TALK LATER.>

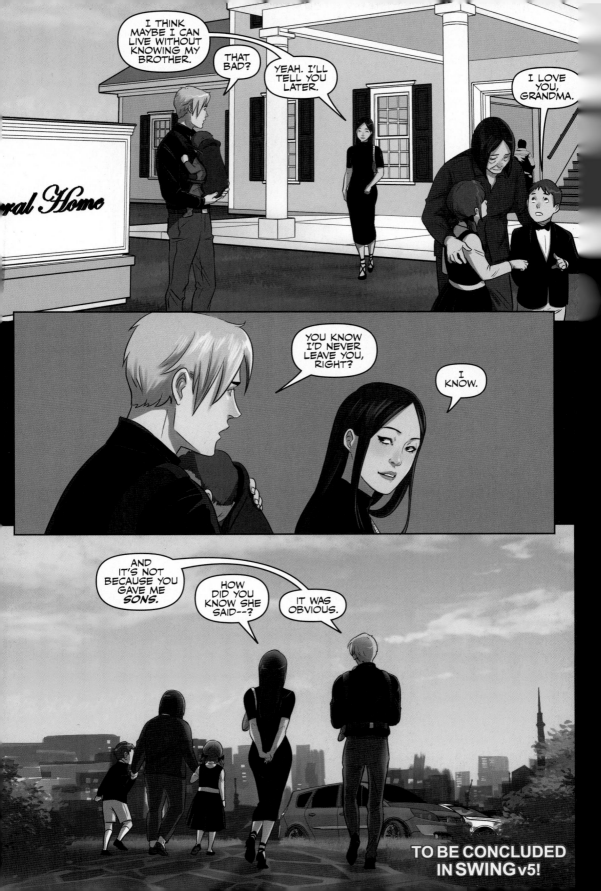

TO BE CONCLUDED IN SWING v5!

SW

VOLUME

THE

20

NG

FIVE
FINALE

22

MATT HAWKINS

is a veteran of the initial Image Comics launch. Matt started his career in comic book publishing in 1993 and has been working with Image as a creator, writer, and executive for over twenty years. President/COO of Top Cow since 1998, Matt has created and written over thirty new franchises for Top Cow and Image including THINK TANK, THE TITHE, STAIRWAY, GOLGOTHA, and APHRODITE IX as well as handling the company's business affairs.

YISHAN LI

is a British/Chinese comic artist currently living in Shanghai. You can see a list of her projects at www.liyishan.com. Yishan Li has been drawing since 1998 and has been published internationally, including USA, France, Germany, Italy, and the UK. She has worked for publishers such as DC and Darkhorse and her last project was the *Buffy: The High School Years* graphic novels.

LINDA SEJIC

is a digital comics artist specializing in an expressive, dynamic art style. Her first major project with Top Cow was WILDFIRE, written by Matt Hawkins, which showcased her unconventional, character-focused technique and established her as an up-and-coming talent. Her critically acclaimed webcomic BLOODSTAIN is currently published in print from Top Cow, and is on its third volume. Linda lives in Croatia with her husband, illustrator Stjepan Sejic.

SEX ED

Welcome to the penultimate volume of Swing! Penultimate is a fancy word we use in comics to mean second to last or "almost last" I think is the true meaning. The point being Volume 5 will be the final book of Dan and Cathy's journey. That doesn't mean "Swing" as a series is done, I am considering doing other series of volumes with different characters and situations. I had a very specific beginning and end in mind for these characters when I first developed them, and it has worked out well. I have run into this with every series I've ever done where I feel like I've told the stories I wanted to tell, and I need to stop so it doesn't feel contrived or not as meaningful. Have you watched shows or read books where the stories start to meander, or it feels like it's "lost" something? This is that commercialization versus creativity battle that is everlasting. When you have a successful series, you want to keep it going for the financial benefit. It's difficult to have a sales success at all and even harder to maintain it, so cancelling or ending a profitable book is always tough to do. The way most publishers get around this is to bring in new creative teams for their long running titles to inject something different or give it new life. This is much harder to do for a creator-owned series like Swing. Often these projects are very personal to the creators, and they could never imagine someone else writing them. I know this has been a frustration for some people who pitch me arcs or projects involving the characters I've created and exclusively written. I don't think I'd ever let anyone else write Think Tank other than Rahsan Ekedal who was my co-creator and artist on that series. Never say never, but you're infinitely more likely to get a job pitching your own original character ideas or pitching arcs on corporately owned books like Spider-Man.

SUNSTONE, NY CLUB, ALLY CARTER

Featured in this volume is Ally from Sunstone and the NY club that Sejic uses in the story. We've had the ongoing video game cross-over which I'll show later in Sex Ed, but this is the first time characters from the two series have met in person and interacted. It's fun to have a little shared universe. We prefer to do it for fun and not make it a requirement, so you don't have to read both books to understand the story.

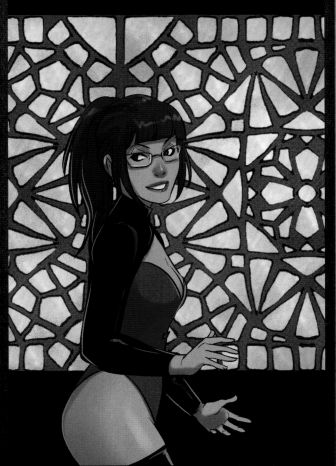

SWING OVERSIZED HARDCOVER

If you've enjoyed the series, I will be doing an oversized hardcover at some point collecting all 5 volumes into one giant book! We tend to do these as a combination of crowdfunding and regular distribution channels. If you want one, should be easy to get. One caveat is I have not paginated out or priced out what that volume would be or cost, so if the costs are high, we may do two hardcover volumes at a lower price point than one massive one

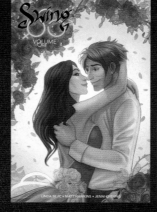

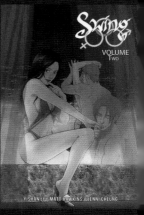

at a higher price point...although I want it to be one! To be determined but hit me up on my social media feeds and let me know your thoughts.

SWING CARD GAME

We are also working on a Swing card game with a board game company so that should be out in 2022-23. I'll talk more about this as it gets closer, but the card game would be multifaceted and playable by couples that don't swing who want to have some sexy fun, couples interested in learning how to swing and by swingers with other swinger couples (either to get to know or to play) and will have vanilla, soft and hardcore play modes. One of the biggest hurdles I see people having in lifestyle is meeting couples they click with. Swingers are like everyone, they're all very different. In this volume I talk about "annual swingers." There are couples out there that go to lifestyle clubs or parties once a year, usually Halloween or New Year's Eve parties to just scratch that itch... they are otherwise monogamous. And if you think the market for this is small, you'd be wrong! Some recent, probably somewhat inflated statistics given the source is a swinger site, show that one in five couples practice some form of ethical non-monogamy. Since about half of swingers won't publicly admit they are, including, ahem, some people I know well, heh. Know thyself!

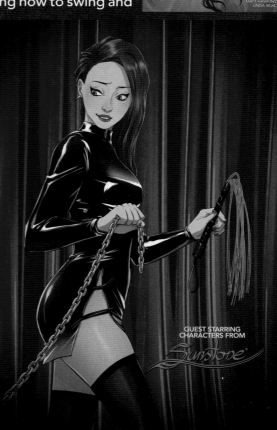

GUEST STARRING
CHARACTERS FROM
Sunstone

RELATIONSHIP ADVICE

It always weirds me out when people ask me for advice on how to deal with their partner. I've been divorced twice, so I'm not sure that qualifies me as an expert. Although I think I know what NOT to do! The best advice I always offer anyone is to be honest, kind, communicative, make a conscious effort to consider your partner in every decision you make and establish agreed upon boundaries. One thing I've tried to do as an adult, meaning very recent, heh, is to be less reactionary and more thoughtful. This applies to everything, but one example is when your partner comes at you angrily, snaps whatever...take a deep breath, use that one second to quickly run through your mind, "What did I do or say that is making them act/react this way?" The answer could be nothing and maybe they just need to vent, but the act of TRYING to empathize is significant. I have often realized too late how easily I could have diffused a situation that I made much worse. If someone is angry, don't ask them why they're angry. Ask what you can do to help them. If they say they need you to do X, Y or Z and it's reasonable then do it. If you can't do it in the immediate, for whatever legitimate reason, tell them when you will. Example being if you're in the middle of writing a work email and your partner asks you to take out the trash, tell them let me finish this email and I will and tell them when (ten minutes, whatever) and then follow through and do it. Nothing makes someone madder than having to repeatedly ask or tell someone to do something and this comes across as nagging when you're the one that created the situation in the first place.

CONVEYING DESIRES/HONESTY

The scene in the lifestyle club where they are beating around what they want when they both want the same thing is something that fascinates me. The point I was trying to make with this scene is even with Dan and Cathy, who have excellent communication and trust, there is always this hesitation and fear to tell our partners what we actually want. The fear of offending them or being rejected often stops us from asking...and when you think about that, it's a bit sad.

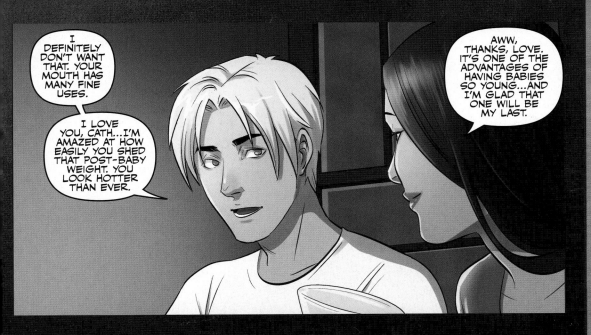

KINDNESS

What I mean by being kind is do all things with your significant other in a loving manner. If you'd like them to lose weight, there are better ways of doing it than being aggressive ("You're fat and need to lose weight.") or passive aggressive ("You know you're not supposed to eat right before bed."). There seems to be a misperception that this is primarily men directed toward women, but as a guy who started dating again in the year before the shutdown (which has led to a new project called Swipe about a middle-aged couple that meets through online dating post-divorce for both) there are a LOT of women I met who had left their husbands and this was at least one factor. What is the right way? It will depend on your specific circumstances, but if it was me and I loved the other person, I'd be encouraging and try and find healthy outdoor activities that they liked to do...with me. Hiking, what have you! I'd cook or treat meals that were healthier and be supportive. And I would try to show by example. People that are overweight know they're overweight, you don't need to tell them. Find healthy and fun things to do as a couple and your relationship will thrive. Again, I'm no expert and not a psychologist, but I have a wealth of life experience and I share it hoping you can pick and choose what may work for you and try it.

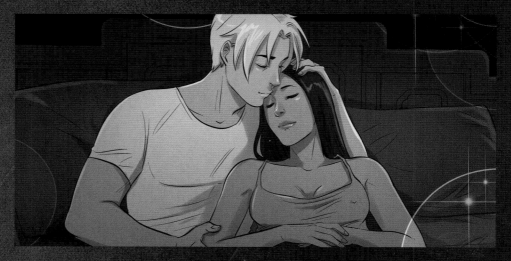

BOUNDARIES

Establishing boundaries of what is and isn't okay is important for any relationship monogamous or not. One couple hit me up on Facebook and asked if I would give my opinion on something. I did, and kind of regretted doing so, but I stand by what I said. Their situation was interesting, it was a heterosexual married couple with kids where the wife did not like that the husband watches porn. My gut reaction was...come on, the vast majority of people watch porn, whether they admit it or not. This situation was more complex, so I had to set aside my own initial feeling and really think about it. The woman in this relationship had set the boundary from the very beginning of their relationship that she would not be okay with him watching porn...ever. The man then dated her for years, they married and had children and flash forward ten years. He feels she's being ridiculous given the prevalence of porn online. I guess since I write books about non-monogamy, he thought I'd back him up. He was stunned when I did not. She set the boundary, he agreed to it and now he wants to change the terms of their agreement...and she does not. They are still married and together as of this writing.

In looking for porn statistics I found a LOT of religious sites vilifying it and they had statistics that were all over the place so not sure where they get their data. And I do agree that porn, like anything, can be a problem for people. I drink WAY too much coffee, it's a huge problem for me and the hole burning in my stomach. Solution? Drink less. If someone is watching porn for ten hours a day, that seems excessive to me and potentially an addiction issue. For me, moderation is the answer to everything, although hard at times to master. If you can't moderate, then you should look at abstaining. Tough to do, but reality is tough.

I've always trusted PsychologyToday.com as a great source of as impartial data as you can get online. This article has some interesting porn statistics and is worth a read:

https://www.psychologytoday.com/us/blog/all-about-sex/201803/surprising-new-data-the-world-s-most-popular-porn-site

MARRIAGE

I've started to think that the construct of marriage needs to be updated somewhat. Most people don't look at marriage for life anymore, even though they might say it in the ceremony. I did vow "Till death do us part" in my first wedding ceremony, but consciously took it out of the second. I think divorce numbers are higher than 50% and likely to grow even higher for a variety of reasons. The marriage for life ideal was created when people got married in their teens, there was no birth control and the average lifespan was in the 30s. It's a lot easier to be married for life when it's less than twenty years and most of those years you're dealing with children. People live a lot longer now and even if you wait until you're 30 to get married, like I did the first time, the average lifespan now is in the seventies. How many of us are radically different after thirty-plus years? I'm 51 at the time I write this and my 21-year-old self is unfathomable to me now. People change. You can either evolve together or apart. Couples that evolve together tend to stay together. Sadly, most don't. I've started to look at my marriages less as failures and more as things that ran their course. My first yielded two beautiful, amazing boys who I love with all my heart. How can I look at the product of their creation as a failure? This could be my own psychological way of dealing with failure, who knows?!? But for my own mental health, trying to look at them through a positive lens is better for me at least. Like jobs and most things, nothing lasts forever. "Till death do us part" is just (at least in my opinion) no longer realistic for most. Do what works for you.

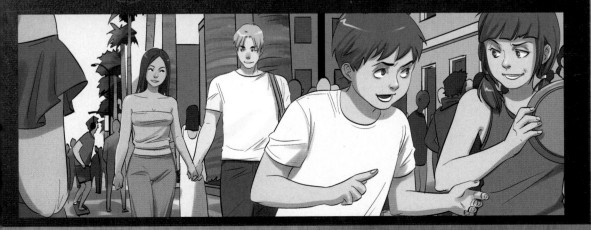

DATE NIGHTS

I've never understood married men who don't have a regular date night with their wives. If you love your partner and want to stay with them, show them a little romance once a week. Try! And there is a wealth of relationship advice columns online, many with lists of date night things that are FREE to do. Use google, it's your friend. I found this one in seconds.

https://www.marriagetrac.com/15-romantic-fun-and-cheap-date-night-ideas-to-try-this-week

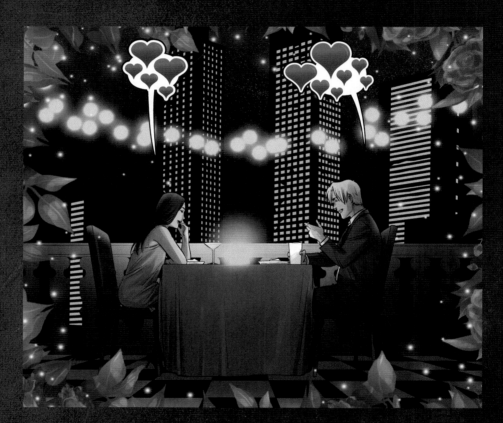

SEX AS PLAY

I never thought of sex as "playful" when I was younger, but I recognize the importance of that as I've gotten older. Swingers refer to sex and hooking up as "play" and clubs refer to the sex areas as "playrooms." It should be fun!

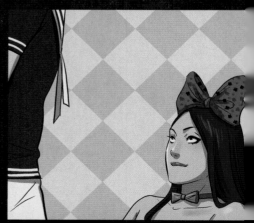

DAN USING BIG WORDS NOW

This is an inside joke. I've intentionally had Dan expand his vocabulary now that he's an "author." My family has made endless fun of me for this, so just me injecting my life experience into the book. I used the word "sophistry" in an argument with my dad and he, a PhD, looked at me and said, "WTF does that mean, is that even a word?"

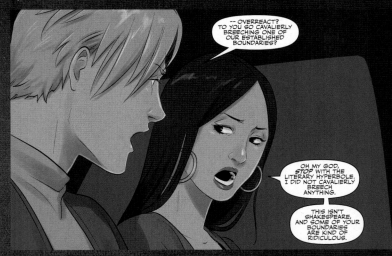

HALLOWEEN, NEW YEAR'S EVE CLUB PARTIES AND HOTEL TAKEOVERS

If you ever wanted to just look around and see what one of these is like, go to one of these parties. I mentioned the annual swingers and lookie-loos above and in the story. These are expected, so if you want to just walk around, have a drink and watch some of the action you can do it at one of these events and have fun! I really love the Halloween parties. Dressing up as a thematic sexy couple is a lot of fun. Yandy.com is a good source for costumes for this.

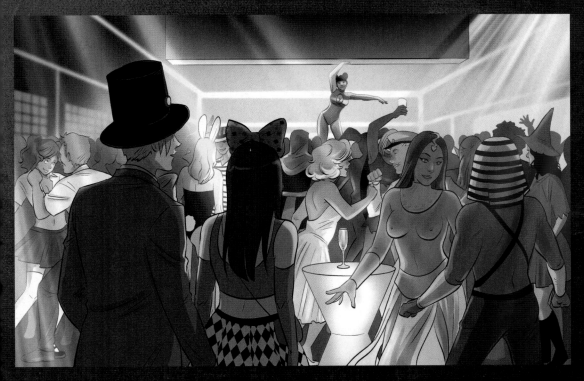

BOOK SIGNINGS

Another example of me using real experience in the book is Dan's signing there at a Barnes and Noble-type store. I've had some amazing signings and I've had ones that no one showed up for. I think this has happened to most comic creators, especially after your first early work gets published. You get excited to have a book with your name on it and want to go celebrate! The reality is it takes time to build an audience and if you only have a limited library of work most people will have never heard of you. Every time I'm in a bookstore or a comic shop and an author or artist is there for a signing, and they are alone I go up and talk to them and buy their book. I stayed for an hour chatting with a guy who wrote a nonfiction book about sailing. I hate sailing. My dad had a sailboat and tried to get me into it, but I get motion sickness and it is ungodly boring to me. Not a knock on it, it's

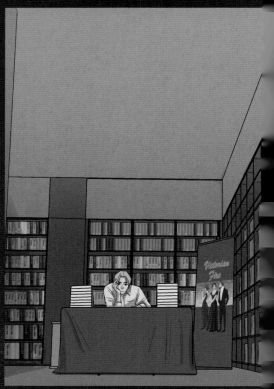

just not for me. Point being, if you see someone like this, think good karma and go chat with them. If you don't want to buy the book that's fine but be nice. Nothing brings people to my convention table more than me talking to someone else. In 1998 when I launched Lady Pendragon at Image, I did a signing in Salt Lake City that was MASSIVE. Biggest one I've ever done, and I signed hundreds of books and I was on the radio there, it really pumped up my ego. I then drove eight hours to Albuquerque for another signing the next day…and after that long of a drive I get there and…zilch. There are a lot of ways to make signings more effective, but this isn't the space for that.

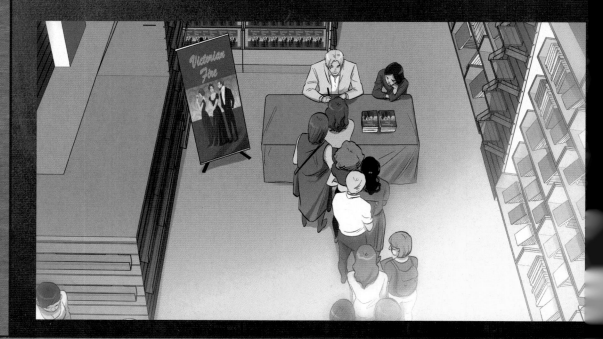

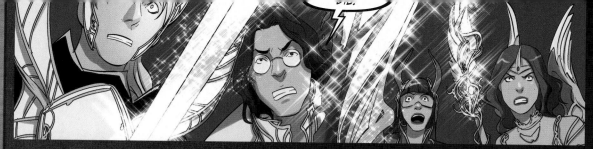

VIDEO GAME CHARACTERS SECTION

As most of you know the true cross-over between Sunstone, Bloodstain and Swing is the game they play. They are all in the same guild and play together as a team. I found a list of gamer terms bouncing around online and cut/pasted the ones I have used for your edutainment.

DAN = HIGH LEVEL WARRIOR TANK

AFK – 'away from keyboard'.

Aggro – when a neutral mob becomes hostile and tries to attack you.

Boss – A tough enemy found at the end of levels or the game.

Lag – the delay between the player's action and the server's response time.

Mob / Mobs – AI/computer-controlled entities.

Noob / n00b – newbie, a person who is new and not skilled enough yet. Usually used in a derogatory manner.

NPC – 'non player character'. Characters who interact with you in game, give you quests or have information/items you need to further the game.

Pwn / Pwned – typo of the word 'owned', used to describe being completely annihilated by an enemy.

Res – to resurrect/revive a teammate.

Tank – a player who keeps all enemies focused on themselves, protecting their teammates. Usually has strong armor and good weapons.

Taunt – using magic, skill or talent to gain the aggro of the mob or boss engaged.

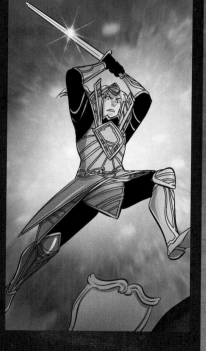

ELLYOLDCOOT- LVL. 98 HEALER
BLOODSTEIN- LVL. 99 PALE KNIGHT (CASHOAR SUPREME)
TOOK OVER A YEAR TO LEVEL UP AND EQUIP HER CHARACTER....STILL NOT DONE
F#$%ING CASHOAR!
BOUGHT EVERYTHING IN A WEEK, MARATHONLEVELED AIDED BY CASSHOP XP BOOSTERS...
OVER 900 USD SPENT
EPEEN VALUE...
PRICELESS!

ALLYCAT-
LVL 97. DARK MAGE
LIIIIIIIIIISA-
LVL. 1 ASSASSIN
(NOOB)
COME OOOON, LET'S GO!
SHUSH, I WANNA SEE WHAT THIS QUEST LOG THING IS ALL ABOUT
BUT....WHY????
TO KNOW THE STORY... DUUUUH!
BUT...BUT...NO ONE CARES ABOUT THE STORY IN AN MMO! YOU GO FROM EXCLAMATION MARK TO EXCLAMATION MARK AND KILL EVERYTHING IN BETWEEN!!!!
YES....BUT WHAT IS OUR MOTIVATION???
SHINIEZ!!!!! IF WE KILL THEM WE GET THEIR STUFF!!!!
SHHH....THIS IS SOME GOOD STUFF HERE!

WRITING SEX SCENES

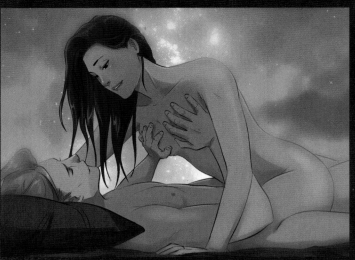

I write these "Marvel-style" which Stan Lee originated as being a loose plot and the artist fleshes it out and then you add the dialogue after. First Linda Sejic and now Yishan Li both lay out and illustrate sex scenes way differently than I would, and I think their versions are better, more sensual and ultimately sexier. The demographics of this book show that 2 out of 3 readers are women. I surround myself with female creators and editors to make sure I do this book without being offensive to women. I think given most men's lifelong relationship to porn and the visual/tactile differences, what is seen from our POV as sexy can be very different from a woman's. I've been a little shocked at times to see some of the sex scenes illustrated as they were more graphic than I would have expected. The crass versus sexy argument is eternal. I routinely ask women in my life their opinions on these things, words used, etc. There's a scene in the book where Cathy is on the bike trying to get back in shape post-pregnancy and she's working some things out in her head. I was worried that her comment that she was bothered by Dan now making more money than her might ring sexist…although one of my wives said this to my face…and both Dan and Cathy are working through their own feelings. Dan's arc with his mother-in-law is one of my favorite subplots in the series that will culminate in the final volume.

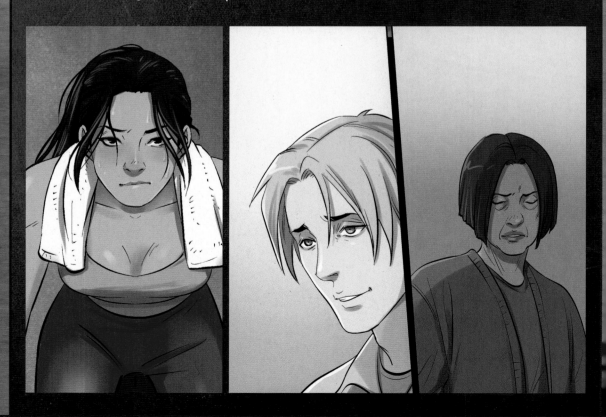

S&M

Definitely more of a Sunstone than Swing thing, but I wanted to include it as most swingers I know have experimented with some bondage, choking, what have you. There are so many resources online about S&M that I won't get into it deeply here, but the hitting of the clit with the belt thing was something I did to a woman. It was an accident, and I didn't know what the hell I was doing, so cautionary tale! That ended that fun for the night. I will say that most people who come up to my convention table who like Sunstone tell me how much they hate Fifty Shades of Grey. I never read the book, although I did see the first film. Most people in that lifestyle do not feel that Fifty Shades properly conveys their ethos which is all about consent and the submissive is actually

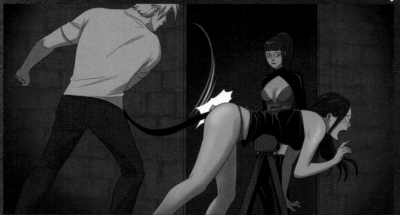

in control. If memory serves, I remember at least one scene where the rich guy took the girl aggressively without her consent. No knock on the book, I know a lot of people like it, it's just not what they see as a fair representation of their lifestyle.

SHIBARI

"In Japanese, 'Shibari' simply means 'to tie'". The contemporary meaning of Shibari describes an ancient Japanese artistic form of rope bondage," from that first link.

I saw this done once and this is one I don't personally get; it looks painful and time-consuming.

Lot of resources online:
https://artofcontemporaryshibari.com/?page_id=29
https://www.shape.com/lifestyle/sex-and-love/shibari-japanese-rope-bondage

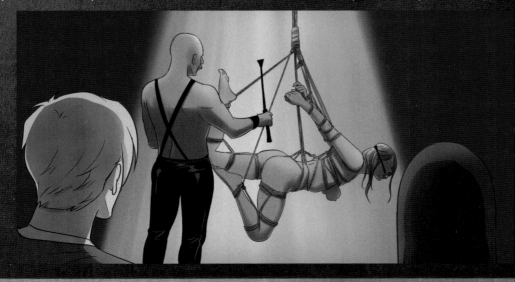

TO EACH THEIR OWN

Whatever your kink might be, part of the fun is discovering what it is. I mentioned above Shibari isn't for me, but I know people that absolutely love it. Let's stop shaming people for their kink. My motto is if it's adults who are consenting, it doesn't involve animals or children and no one is getting hurt, go for it. S&M pain to me isn't someone getting "hurt" it's a pleasure/pain threshold that they are toying with voluntarily. It was also fun to show Dan and Cathy experiment with it and decide it wasn't for them. When I first pitched that to Sejic I thought he'd say no but he loved the idea. Again, it hits the center of the ideal that everyone is different and whatever kink you might be into (given my usual constraints) is okay and you shouldn't be shamed by it.

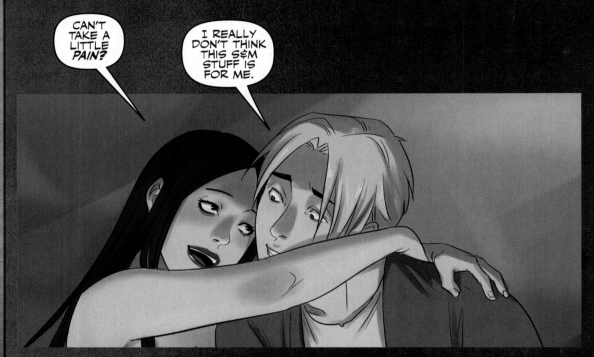

And that's it for this volume and edition of Sex Ed! I truly hope you enjoyed it and maybe even learned something. Word of mouth is the best way to sell books and get new readers, so if you did enjoy it please spread the word. I am reachable, although please be patient, on my social media feeds and will try to answer your questions if you have some. And don't come to me for advice on relationships! There are significantly better resources at your disposal, so make use of them.

Carpe Diem,

Matt Hawkins
August 1, 2021
Twitter: @topcowmatt | http://www.facebook.com/selfloathingnarcissist

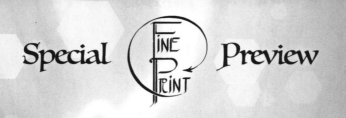

Prologue

The butterfly
that started
the storm

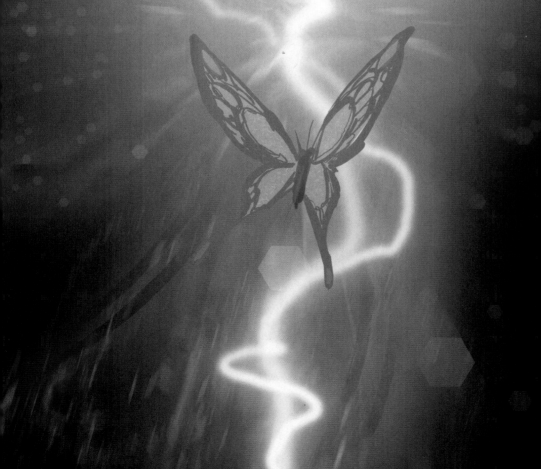

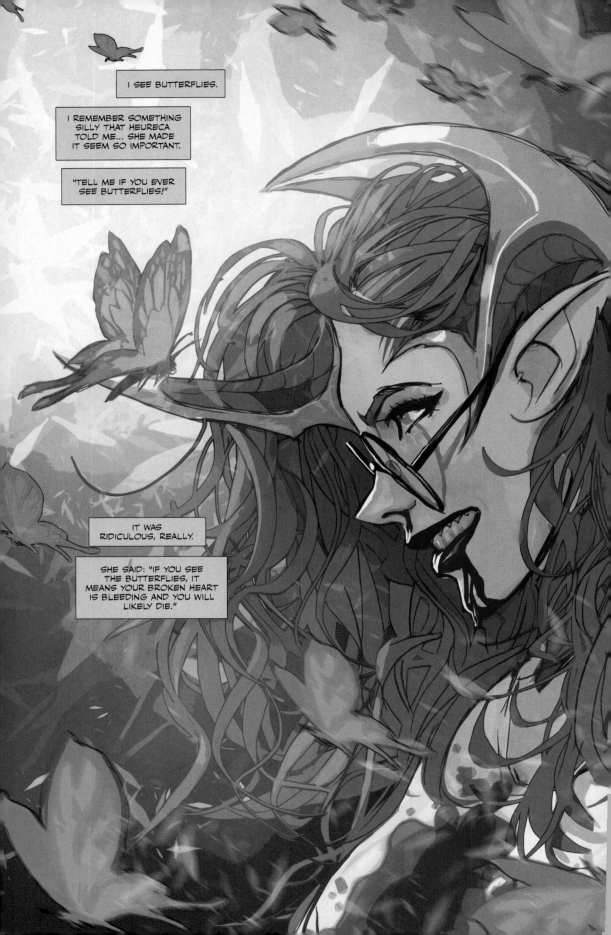

I SEE BUTTERFLIES.

I REMEMBER SOMETHING SILLY THAT HEURECA TOLD ME... SHE MADE IT SEEM SO IMPORTANT.

"TELL ME IF YOU EVER SEE BUTTERFLIES!"

IT WAS RIDICULOUS, REALLY.

SHE SAID: "IF YOU SEE THE BUTTERFLIES, IT MEANS YOUR BROKEN HEART IS BLEEDING AND YOU WILL LIKELY DIE."

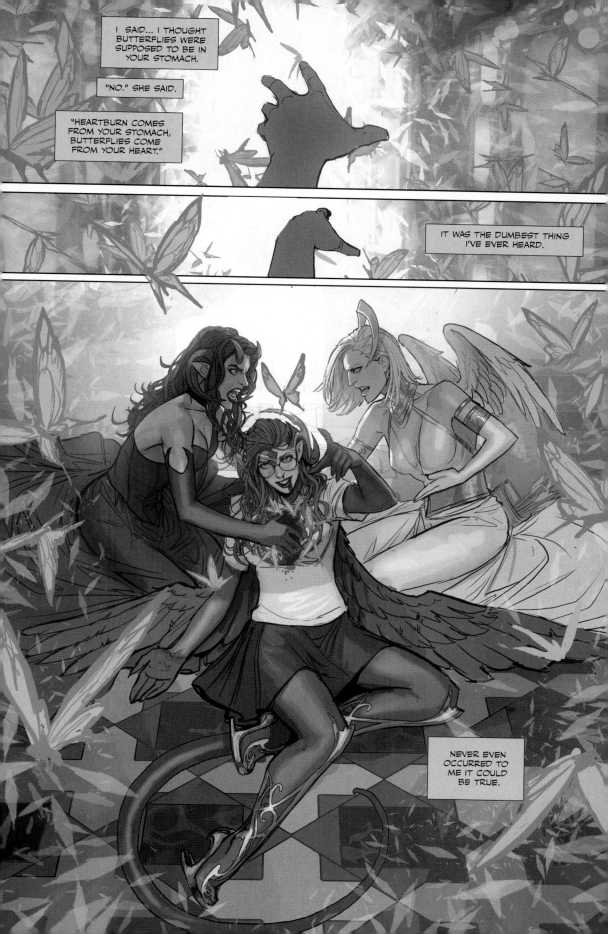

I SAID... I THOUGHT BUTTERFLIES WERE SUPPOSED TO BE IN YOUR STOMACH.

"NO." SHE SAID.

"HEARTBURN COMES FROM YOUR STOMACH, BUTTERFLIES COME FROM YOUR HEART."

IT WAS THE DUMBEST THING I'VE EVER HEARD.

NEVER EVEN OCCURRED TO ME IT COULD BE TRUE.

AS THE DELIRIUM KICKS IN I REMEMBER THAT OTHER THING ABOUT BUTTERFLIES...
THE BUTTERFLY EFFECT— YOU KNOW, WHERE ONE FLAPS ITS WINGS ON ONE SIDE OF THE WORLD AND STARTS A CHAIN REACTION THAT CAUSES A HURRICANE ON THE OTHER SIDE OF THE WORLD.
WELL. HERE I AM DYING AT THE EYE OF THAT HURRICANE...
AND MY LAST THOUGHTS ARE OF THAT BUTTERFLY THAT STARTED IT ALL.

A STORM OF A LIFETIME BIRTHED BY ONE...
SIMPLE
INNOCENT...
...FLAP.
HI, I'M MERRYL! CAN I HELP YOU?

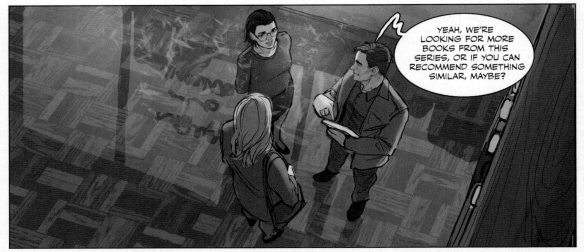

YEAH, WE'RE LOOKING FOR MORE BOOKS FROM THIS SERIES, OR IF YOU CAN RECOMMEND SOMETHING SIMILAR, MAYBE?

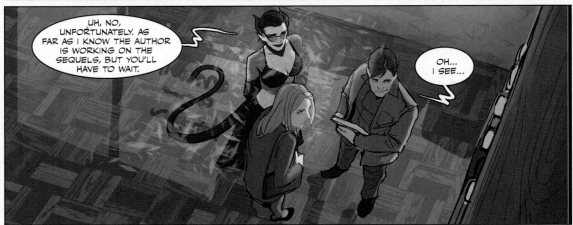

UH, NO, UNFORTUNATELY. AS FAR AS I KNOW THE AUTHOR IS WORKING ON THE SEQUELS, BUT YOU'LL HAVE TO WAIT.

OH... I SEE...

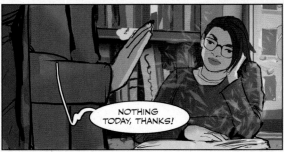

NOTHING TODAY, THANKS!

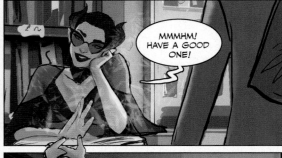

MMMHM! HAVE A GOOD ONE!

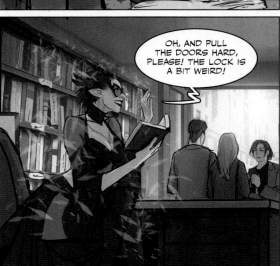

OH, AND PULL THE DOORS HARD, PLEASE! THE LOCK IS A BIT WEIRD!

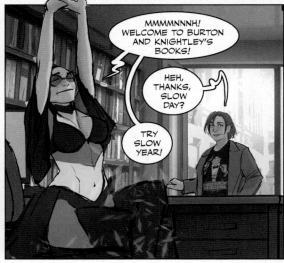

MMMMNNNH! WELCOME TO BURTON AND KNIGHTLEY'S BOOKS!

HEH, THANKS, SLOW DAY?

TRY SLOW YEAR!

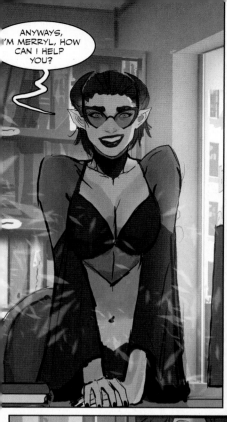

ANYWAYS, I'M MERRYL, HOW CAN I HELP YOU?

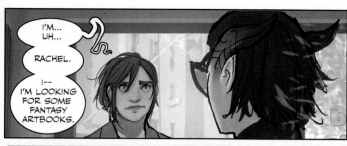

I'M... UH...

RACHEL.

I-- I'M LOOKING FOR SOME FANTASY ARTBOOKS.

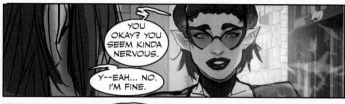

YOU OKAY? YOU SEEM KINDA NERVOUS.

Y--EAH... NO. I'M FINE.

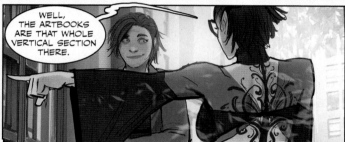

WELL, THE ARTBOOKS ARE THAT WHOLE VERTICAL SECTION THERE.

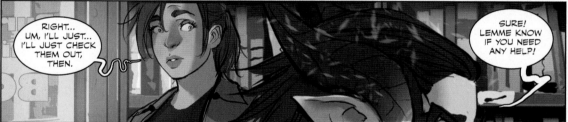

RIGHT... UM, I'LL JUST... I'LL JUST CHECK THEM OUT, THEN.

SURE! LEMME KNOW IF YOU NEED ANY HELP!

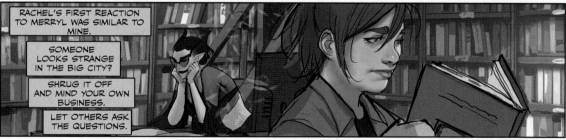

RACHEL'S FIRST REACTION TO MERRYL WAS SIMILAR TO MINE.

SOMEONE LOOKS STRANGE IN THE BIG CITY?

SHRUG IT OFF AND MIND YOUR OWN BUSINESS.

LET OTHERS ASK THE QUESTIONS.

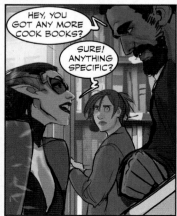

HEY, YOU GOT ANY MORE COOK BOOKS?

SURE! ANYTHING SPECIFIC?

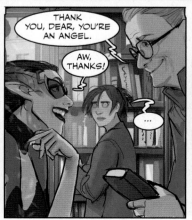

THANK YOU, DEAR, YOU'RE AN ANGEL.

AW, THANKS!

...

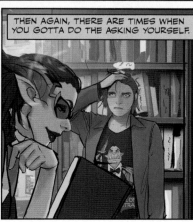

THEN AGAIN, THERE ARE TIMES WHEN YOU GOTTA DO THE ASKING YOURSELF.

HI, ME AGAIN!
OH, HEY, FOUND ANYTHING INTERESTING?
NOT ON THE BOOKSHELVES.
SORRY?
WELL NO ONE ELSE IS ASKING ABOUT IT, SO I MUST BE THE ONLY PERSON HERE OUT OF THE LOOP...
SO, IS THE STORE DOING SOME KIND OF A BOOK PROMOTION OR SOMETHING?
ONDUCTOR OF THE ORCESTRA
HERE? NAH. WE CAN'T EVEN ARRANGE SIGNINGS WITH AUTHORS THESE DAYS.
RIGHT... RIGHT... WHAT'S WITH THE COSPLAY THEN?
THE WHAT?
THE WHOLE HORNS AND TAIL THING?
I THOUGHT THAT WAS LIKE A PROMOTIONAL STUNT FOR A BOOK OR SOMETHING?
MY HORNS AND...
WAIT! YOU CAN SEE THESE?
I MEAN, THEY'RE PRETTY LARGE,
ALSO HOW IS THAT TAIL MOVING LIKE THAT?

RIGHT, HOLD THAT THOUGHT.
OKAY EVERYONE THERE'S AN EMERGENCY AND WE'RE CLOSING EARLY TODAY.
WHAT KIND OF EMERGENCY?
WE FOUND TYPOS IN A DICTIONARY. EVERYBODY OUT!
NOT YOU!
ALSO, WHAT ARE YOU DOING, THAT'S NOT SANTA'S BEARD!
TUG
TUG
THIS... THIS IS A REAL TAIL!!!
YES, AND BEFORE YOU START PULLING ON THEM AS WELL, SO ARE THE HORNS!
CONDUCTOR OF THE ORCESTRA
I...WH...
UH...
WHO ARE YOU?

ME, I'M MERRYL ALARIS. I'M WHAT YOUR PEOPLE WOULD CALL A SUCCUBUS.
YOU'RE SHITTING ME!
YOU'RE AN ACTUAL DEMON!?
CONDUCTOR OF THE ORCESTR
OKAY, I'D REALLY APPRECIATE IT IF YOU DIDN'T CALL ME A DEMON.
IT'S A BIT OF A PET PEEVE, OKAY?
MY KIND IS CALLED CUBI.
SHIT, I'M SORRY, IT'S JUST...
THIS IS ALL KINDS OF SURREAL RIGHT NOW.
LIKE... I'M A FANTASY WRITER, I WRITE ABOUT FANTASY CREATURES, AND THE LAST THING I EXPECTED WHEN I GOT OUT OF THE BED TODAY IS TO SEE ONE IN SOME RANDOM ASS BOOKSTORE!
AAAND NOW I'VE GONE AND CALLED YOU A FANTASY CREATURE...
HAH! CERTAINLY BEATS CALLING ME A DEMON!

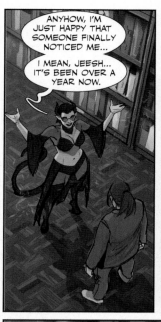

ANYHOW, I'M JUST HAPPY THAT SOMEONE FINALLY NOTICED ME...

I MEAN, JEESH... IT'S BEEN OVER A YEAR NOW.

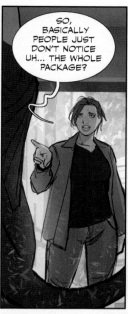

SO, BASICALLY PEOPLE JUST DON'T NOTICE UH... THE WHOLE PACKAGE?

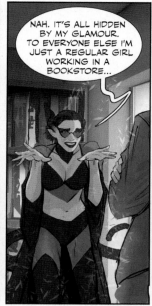

NAH. IT'S ALL HIDDEN BY MY GLAMOUR. TO EVERYONE ELSE I'M JUST A REGULAR GIRL WORKING IN A BOOKSTORE...

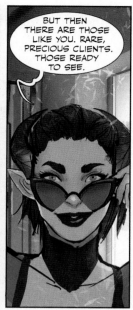

BUT THEN THERE ARE THOSE LIKE YOU. RARE, PRECIOUS CLIENTS. THOSE READY TO SEE.

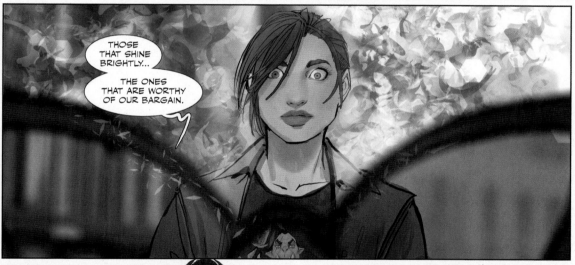

THOSE THAT SHINE BRIGHTLY...

THE ONES THAT ARE WORTHY OF OUR BARGAIN.

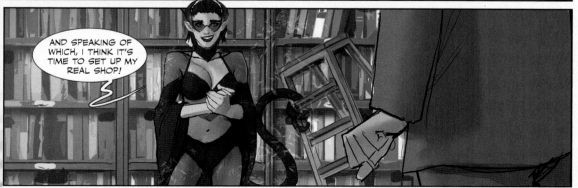

AND SPEAKING OF WHICH, I THINK IT'S TIME TO SET UP MY REAL SHOP!

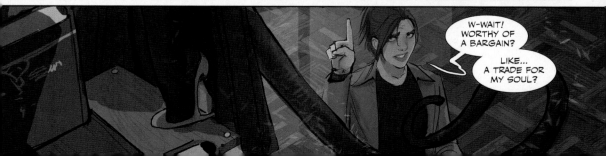

W-WAIT! WORTHY OF A BARGAIN?

LIKE... A TRADE FOR MY SOUL?

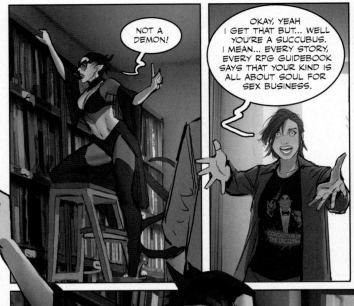

NOT A DEMON!

OKAY, YEAH I GET THAT BUT... WELL YOU'RE A SUCCUBUS. I MEAN... EVERY STORY, EVERY RPG GUIDEBOOK SAYS THAT YOUR KIND IS ALL ABOUT SOUL FOR SEX BUSINESS.

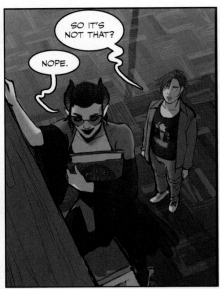

SO IT'S NOT THAT?

NOPE.

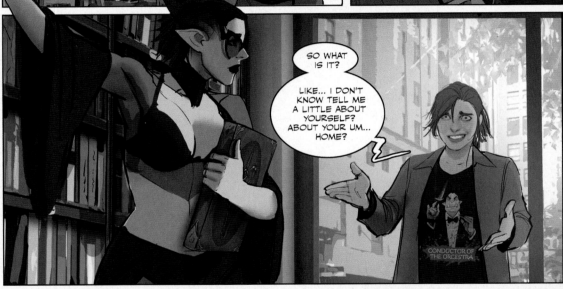

SO WHAT IS IT?

LIKE... I DON'T KNOW TELL ME A LITTLE ABOUT YOURSELF? ABOUT YOUR UM... HOME?

CONDUCTOR OF THE ORCESTRA

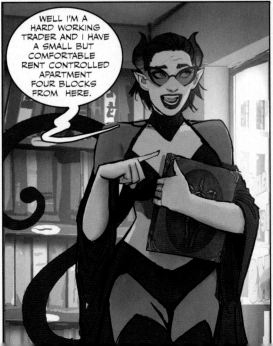

WELL I'M A HARD WORKING TRADER AND I HAVE A SMALL BUT COMFORTABLE RENT CONTROLLED APARTMENT FOUR BLOCKS FROM HERE.

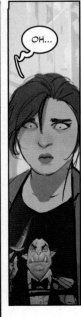

OH...

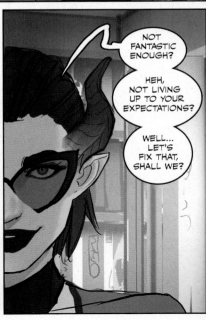

NOT FANTASTIC ENOUGH?

HEH, NOT LIVING UP TO YOUR EXPECTATIONS?

WELL... LET'S FIX THAT, SHALL WE?

LIKE I SAID, I'M A BIT OF A BLUE COLLAR WORKER.
CONDUCTOR OF THE ORCEST
BUT IF YOU WANT GLAMOUR...
IF YOU WANT BLISS AND MAGIC...
WELL I GUESS WE COULD WORK SOMETHING OUT!
Coming Soon

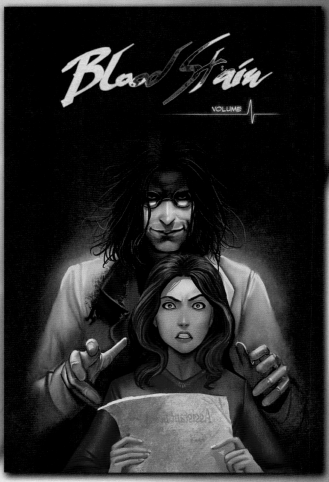

**VOLUME 1
DIAMOND CODE:
OCT150604**

Blood Stain
VOLUME
LINDA SEJIC
Blood Stain
VOLUME

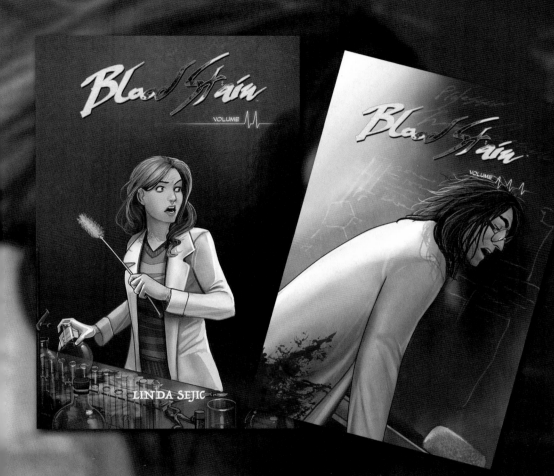

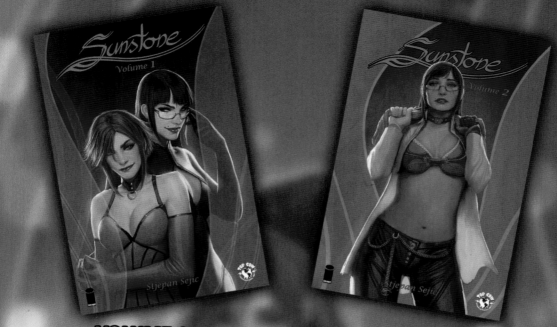

VOLUME 1
DIAMOND CODE:
OCT140613
ISBN: 9781632152121

VOLUME 2
DIAMOND CODE:
FEB150538
ISBN: 9781632152299

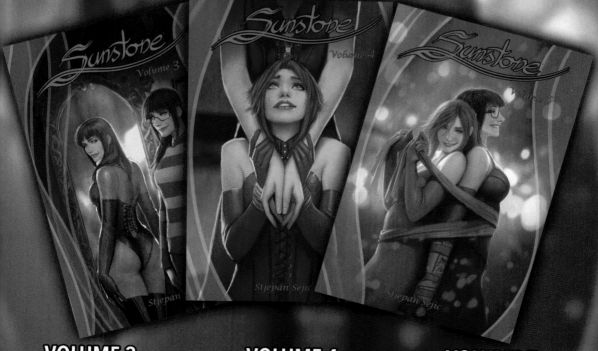

VOLUME 3
DIAMOND CODE:
JUN150583
ISBN: 9781632153999

VOLUME 4
DIAMOND CODE:
OCT150579
ISBN: 9781632156099

VOLUME 5
DIAMOND CODE:
MAY160731
ISBN: 9781632157249

The classic tale of Greek mythology,
but 100 percent more awkwardly relatable.
punderworld™
Linda Sejic
AVAILABLE NOW
TOP COW PRODUCTIONS, INC.
image
DIAMOND CODE: JUN210157 ISBN: 978-1-5343-2072-7

The Top Cow essentials checklist:

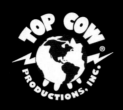

Aphrodite IX: Rebirth, **Volume 1**
(ISBN: 978-1-60706-828-0)

Blood Stain, **Volume 1**
(ISBN: 978-1-63215-544-3)

Bonehead, **Volume 1**
(ISBN: 978-1-5343-0664-6)

Cyber Force: Awakening, **Volume 1**
(ISBN: 978-1-5343-0980-7)

The Clock, **Volume 1**
(ISBN: 978-1-5343-1611-9)

The Darkness: Origins, **Volume 1**
(ISBN: 978-1-60706-097-0)

Death Vigil, **Volume 1**
(ISBN: 978-1-63215-278-7)

Dissonance, **Volume 1**
(ISBN: 978-1-5343-0742-1)

Eclipse, **Volume 1**
(ISBN: 978-1-5343-0038-5)

Eden's Fall, **Volume 1**
(ISBN: 978-1-5343-0065-1)

The Freeze, **OGN**
(ISBN: 978-1-5343-1211-1)

God Complex, **Volume 1**
(ISBN: 978-1-5343-0657-8)

Infinite Dark, **Volume 1**
(ISBN: 978-1-5343-1056-8)

Paradox Girl, Volume 1
(ISBN: 978-1-5343-1220-3)

Port of Earth, **Volume 1**
(ISBN: 978-1-5343-0646-2)

Postal, **Volume 1**
(ISBN: 978-1-63215-342-5)

Stairway Anthology
(ISBN: 978-1-5343-1702-4)

Sugar, **Volume 1**
(ISBN: 978-1-5343-1641-7)

Sunstone, **Volume 1**
(ISBN: 978-1-63215-212-1)

Swing, **Volume 1**
(ISBN: 978-1-5343-0516-8)

Symmetry, **Volume 1**
(ISBN: 978-1-63215-699-0)

The Tithe, **Volume 1**
(ISBN: 978-1-63215-324-1)

Think Tank, **Volume 1**
(ISBN: 978-1-60706-660-6)

Vindication, **OGN**
(ISBN: 978-1-5343-1237-1)

Warframe, **Volume 1**
(ISBN: 978-1-5343-0512-0)

Witchblade 2017, **Volume 1**
(ISBN: 978-1-5343-0685-1)

For more ISBN and ordering information on our latest collections go to:
www.topcow.com
Ask your retailer about our catalogue of collected editions,
digests, and hard covers or check the listings at:
Barnes and Noble, Amazon.com,
and other fine retailers.

To find your nearest comic shop go to:
www.comicshoplocator.com